Flesh and Bone

Flesh and Bone

Stories

Cydney Chadwick

Avec Books
Penngrove

Grateful acknowledgment to the editors of the journals (both online and print) and anthologies in which some of these stories first appeared: *The Attic, Blaze, Central Park, The Chicago Literary Review, First Intensity, Five Fingers Review, The Gertrude Stein Awards in Innovative American Poetry 1994-1995, The Illinois Review, Lingo, Lucy House of Prose, The Minnesota Review, New American Writing, Non, Out of Everywhere, Potepoetzine, Situation, SPAD, Sugarmule, Texture, Tight, Tinfish, The Washington Review, Volt* and *ZYZZYVA*.

Thanks to Mark Wallace, Stephen-Paul Martin and Christopher Reiner for their editorial comments on these texts. C.C.

The author would also like to thank the California Arts Council for a creative writing fellowship that allowed her to complete some of these stories.

ISBN:1-880713-28-4
Library of Congress
Control Number: 2001093329

Cover images by Ben E. Watkins
Cover design by Colleen Barclay

Avec Books
P. O. Box 1059
Penngrove, CA 94951

for Angela Chadwick

CONTENTS

Irritants

"That we are change-
able and temporary, burning down like fire, but slower (usually)."
—Laura Moriarty

THE EYES BLINK. An eyelash is loosened from its base, hovering momentarily before it drops. The eyes open and the lash falls onto the cornea.

For some this would be noticeable, but for those who wear contact lenses, the eyes become somewhat desensitized. When the eyes blink again, the pressure from the upper lid forces the lash under the lower one. The man rubs the eye with the back of his hand, moving the lash between the fold of the inner lid and the eyeball. The man thinks his contact lenses may need cleaning, or perhaps a cat hair lodged itself inside his eye.

Later in the day the man feels a twinge and thinks there might indeed be a hair from the cat caught between the lens and his eyeball. It happens sometimes—hairs from the calico drift into the atmosphere as she is being brushed. He pulls the skin around his eye taut, stares into a mirror, blinks several times and carefully moves a tissue twisted into a point around the circle of the contact lens. This makes his eye itch slightly, and causes tiny red veins to pop out in the whiteness. The man finds nothing. The tissue leaves minuscule fibers on his eyeball, which the man does not feel.

Several hours later, he still senses an irritant, pops out his right lens and holds it up to the light. There is nothing but the usual mucins accumulated from day-to-day wear, which form a cloudy ring, rinsed away with solution every evening and built up again the following day.

While the man sleeps, mircoorganisms that adhere to the eyelash are rapidly multiplying, for the lash is still nestled in the warmth of the man's lower lid. This triggers macrophages to begin eating and partially digesting the invading organisms—which in turn alerts the man's T and B cells to spring into action. But they may not be successful. The man might be unaware of his condition for several days, until he wakes up one morning to find his eye red and swollen, has to call an ophthalmologist, take an antibiotic prescription while refraining from wearing his contact lenses—resorting to glasses with an out-of-date prescription. Or the antibodies may render the invaders harmless, and the eyelash will resurface on the eyeball, where the man will finally feel its presence, see it reflected in his eye's mirrored image, take a tissue and dislodge it, glancing at the small amount of mucus on the lash and think that the body is good at dispelling things.

On Tuesday the man again feels the lash, rolls a Kleenex into a point and removes it. *I thought there was something.*

It is an uneventful week. He closes a deal he thought would close, and receives a parking ticket. Saturday morning he is in gray sweatpants, stretching on the living room floor, before going to the park to play a game of doubles. As he is on his hands and knees loosening up his hamstrings, the calico comes into the room, rushes over and bites him on the left buttock. *Christ* the man shouts, frightening the cat and causing her to slink from the room. The man pulls down his sweatpants and sees two teeth marks, but the skin is not broken. He grabs his racket and walks over to the park.

At the courts he sees his partner and a player from the opposing team, but instead of the fourth there is a woman warming up. He is annoyed. He does not like to play tennis against women. If he plays full out he could be perceived as a heel, but if he eases up she might get some shots past him and make him look foolish.

At four-all in the first set both teams are at the net when the woman drills him with a forehand volley. Her hand flies out, palm up, the international sign of apology, that the shot was not meant. The man's first impulse is to fire a ball back at her, but she is not ugly. *No problem*, he smiles. The ball's impact continues to sting his abdomen as he runs back to the baseline to receive serve. He now faces a dilemma: if he plays harder and directs his shots toward the woman, the three of them will think he is upset over an accidental shot from a female. However, of the two across the net, she is the weaker player, and basic doubles strategy calls for hitting the ball to the weaker player's side of the court. Nonetheless, the man cannot regain his concentration, begins spraying his shots and he and his partner lose the set 6 games to 4. Two of the players cannot stay for another set so, peeved about losing, the man jogs slowly home.

That evening he is at dinner with two of his friends, a married couple, who bring up something political. The man finds words coming out of his mouth, phrases the couple undoubtedly agree with. When he stops speaking he wonders why he uttered those things; he doesn't think he believes them. Or does he? In recent months he has found himself doing this more and more frequently—saying things he may not actually think. He does not feel pressured to impress the individuals he is speaking to; on the contrary, they are close and accepting friends. At certain times the man feels like there isn't much there. There is a body and there is language. There is an arm holding a racket that strikes a tennis ball, there is speech that closes deals, a hand that encloses others after agreements.

Sometimes when the man goes out for a long period of time he returns home to find the cat has shit in his shoe. She began to do this just after kittenhood, when he was not used to having a cat and would sometimes forget to change the litterbox. He learned that cats are very fastidious animals who do not like digging in soiled litter. Now he is careful about making sure there is a clean box before he leaves for work, or other prolonged activities. Nonetheless, when he forgets to close his closet, she sometimes goes inside, finds a dress shoe and defecates—maybe to spite him for being left for so long. She has never chosen athletic shoes; perhaps finding the faint but lingering odor of sweat repugnant. The man has, after forgetting to close the closet, discarded several pairs of wing-tips, loafers and even a pair of almost new Lorenzo Banfis. It has occurred to him to keep the shoes and get rid of the cat, but no matter how many times he cleaned the footwear, it would do no good. Although he knows that viruses and bacteria do not live long, and most are killed by soap, alcohol, or time, the idea would always remain with the shoes. If he were to get rid of the cat, though, he would be the kind of person who abandons animals and secretly desires to hit women with tennis balls.

The man owns stock. Most are fairly conservative but since he is relatively young, unmarried and without children to support, he can afford to take some risks.

He is working at home and turns on a news channel after the Dow closes for the day. His tech stock has gone up thirty percent. He has just made around thirty-thousand dollars, will call his broker first thing in the morning and tell him to sell. He feels jubilant, euphoric, leaps into the air and screams, *yes!* He comes down on the cat's tail—it in turn leaps into the air, screeches and comes down on the man's calf, digging its claws into his skin before rushing off wild-eyed with a voluminous tail, to take refuge under the man's bed. He pulls up his pant leg and sees two red lines, welts beginning to form, edged with drops of blood. He takes a towel, rubbing alcohol and swabs at the area.

Several days later the wounds have scabbed over, but are slightly painful, and the skin around them is warmer than the surrounding skin. He has been very conscious of the leg. If the heat and pain persist he will go to a physician and get antibiotics, for over the past few days he imagines he can feel silent, tiny microbes moving to-and-fro inside him. He speculates whether or not this could be possible, that such sensory phenomenon can exist, if something like that can make itself felt from so deep inside a physiology.

The man feels hot and his head pounds. The thermostat must be broken because it only reads sixty-five degrees. Although it snowed several days before and gray slush still lingers in drainage ditches, the man flings open a window and leans into the cold air. It is a clear, crisp day with strong winds gusting from the east. Some of his papers blow to the floor and they catch the calico's attention. She watches the path of several more papers as they scatter to the floor, then pads across the room, jumps on the window sill and looks at the man. He believes he can hear the blood moving through his temples. It is hurting him. His eyes water from the cold and wind, but he continues to lean through the window frame, enjoying the invigorating elements, their cooling and potentially numbing effect. While he surveys the familiar city street, he squints to make the stinging of his eyes bearable as the wind hits his lenses and his corneas dry out—air wicking away moisture from the optical membranes. This causes the lachrymal glands embedded in his eye sockets to release a salt-and-enzyme-containing fluid. Involuntary antidote.

Mists

IN HIS ROOM he is a famous poet. Publishers clamor for his manuscripts, he has the admiration of his peers and is a shoo-in to win all the prizes.

When he ventures down the stairs to his mailbox he is still a famous poet, but while out on the street amidst others he is not quite as renowned. The further he gets from his apartment the less well-known he is. If he leaves town he finds himself an obscure shell of a person, ambitionless, directionless, wandering the streets of an unfamiliar city.

While in public places she is a young woman—tall, redheaded and statuesque. Both men and woman admire her luscious sexuality, and those around her cannot help but be seduced—if she so chooses. It is only when she returns home after cocktail parties that she can look in the mirror. She sees a lined face, a turned down mouth and cynical eyes. She knows she is only a few years away from becoming eligible for senior citizen discounts, and will continue on this path devoid of sexual attention. The following morning, she lies in bed, hungover, unable to think of a good reason to get up. It takes several days before she can shake off her depression, rise from her bed and go out again.

The woman buys some cloth and nails it to the maple frame of her one remaining mirror. But one evening after coming home intoxicated, she rips it off, confronts her image, spends the next several days in bed, re-nails the fabric to the mirror's frame and goes out for cocktails.

An old age pensioner sitting on a park bench is convinced he is young and virile, smiles happily to himself. From his bench he ogles women and girls, convinced they want him—that is why they pass by in colored bras, or running singlets and shorts. They go around again and again, flaunting themselves on skates, on bikes, or while jogging. Sometimes thoughts creep into his mind, dark, ugly thoughts—they are not even aware he is there, are only in the park to exercise, and he is an old man on a bench, but these ruminations are too scary and he drives them from his mind.

Two women decide to meet for lunch after not having seen each other for thirty years. They discuss their families, hobbies, what has happened to old friends, and after a time recall their youth. *Remember,* one woman says, *that terrible car accident I was in? You passed by several minutes later and stopped to help us.* The other woman's eyes grow wide and disbelieving, for it was she and her husband who had been in the car accident. Her friend had not been present that summer night, had, in fact, been visiting her aunt in another state. She and her fiancé were towed out of the field by the farmer who owned the property. *I still have a scar from the accident,* the woman who'd been away during the crash says, rubbing away a bit of makeup to reveal a small but distinct mark on her cheek.

A man is convinced creditors are after him, although he settles all his monthly bills and has a perfect record of payment. He hurries through the streets, avoiding eye contact with all, becomes terror-stricken when he spies men in black shirts who could be loan sharks. Someone else might be after him too, disgruntled postal workers, or the waitress in this coffee shop, disappointed and angry at men, who is just dying to empty the contents of her coffeepot into his crotch. The man is convinced he is enveloped in a dark and swirling cloud of doom—although those who know him think the facts of his life make it an existence that must be pleasant and easy.

There are those who believe we go through life enshrouded in a mist. For some this mist is dark, for others light, and we move through the world seeing through its semi-opaque parameters. The perceptions and beliefs we hold to be true become damaged as we inevitably become emeshed in the mists of others. This we find hardly bearable. It causes us terror, it makes us mean.

Flight

YOU STAND ON your tiptoes, feet wobbling on the unsteady surface of your bed, face pressed against the wall and raised to the spaces between the metal slats. Next door, a man is smoking marijuana, blowing his residual smoke through the shared heater vent.

You have been secretly partaking in the man's Friday afternoon ritual for some months, having decided that because you don't purchase or light it, your contact with the substance is merely happenstance.

When you first detected the smell, you got up from your desk and sniffed around your bedroom, puzzled. The following Friday you again noticed the odor, and the following week, and the week after that. During a Friday afternoon that was going rather badly, you again caught the scent of marijuana's sweetness, hurried to your bedroom in time to see tiny trails of smoke drift up toward your ceiling and disappear. Instinctively, you climbed onto your bed, pressed your face to the vent and breathed deeply, pleasantly surprised afterward that you'd been in close enough contact with the substance to now feel different.

You have deduced that the man's ritual always takes place on Fridays because he gets home several hours earlier than his wife.

You also know that the man smokes his marijuana in the bathroom, as you can hear the whirring of his bathroom fan, his turning on the shower when he is finished. Perhaps the shower steam aids in dissipating the smell, which in turn helps him to deceive his wife into thinking he is not under any influence.

When you breathed through the vent for the first time, you no longer felt like working, and wandered around the apartment, picking things up and putting them down again. Finally, you went out, walking in the early onset of winter darkness. You noted, with heightened interest, people hurried and tense, people yelling at one another over parking places, people trying to get their errands done before the shops closed, people stumbling, people swearing.

You didn't know what you wanted to do, have a drink, or a cup of tea, or go to the magazine shop and browse through journals, secure in the fact that the proprietor would be smoking a cigarette and would not engage you in conversation.

You walked by a large storefront, pausing to look at a strange set of tea pots: a pig, an elephant, the water designed to pour from its upturned trunk, a teapot made in the shape of a large green lizard. Unable to discern if they were charming or ridiculous, you nonetheless went inside.

Soon this becomes your weekly ritual: to stand atop your bed inhaling deeply, to walk the streets in the dissipating light, to wander through the many antique shops that comprise this part of the city, imagining the people who once owned the silver-plated oriental jewelry adorned with dancing girls, the crumbling and pointed women's shoes, the austere walnut tables, the mothball scented clothing. It becomes a game, to conjure up what the owners looked like, how old they were, their circumstances and eras. It makes you think of ghostliness, of the dead, and in your present state you like this.

On the Friday afternoon following Thanksgiving, the man blows marijuana through the heater vent earlier than usual. You sprint across the room and leap onto your bed, expanding your lungs. You suspect his wife has gone out for a time and it is now or never for him. When he is finished you hear the familiar rush of shower spray.

Outdoors the light hurts your eyes, and there are so many people roaming about that you begin to feel nervous, consider returning home, but keep moving toward your destination.

The stores have been well-stocked for the holiday season, proprietors well aware that one person's junk constitutes another's rare find. Near a jewelry case you come upon a silver oval containing a photograph of an ice skater caught in a split jump, balletic and staring into the camera. Judging from the high skating boots and flared skirt, you guess the photograph was taken in the 1930s or 40s.

You recall several minutes from long ago, preserved on eight millimeter film somewhere, by someone now old, or perhaps dead. You gained speed and jumped, suspending yourself at the apex, and when you came back down to the ice, you once again gathered momentum and leaped, trying to remain aloft, and again came back down, stroking the hard, white surface with deep edges, moving faster, and again took off. It was easy to jump too high at that altitude, but there was nothing better than being airborne and rotating.

Today, that form you were once inside of, unable to imagine any other, has vanished, as has that boundary between yourself and the world. All these years later you are in an antique shop at the beginning of the Christmas holidays, in an altered state, holding a silver-plated oval of an ice skater, while trying to remain unobtrusive.

This is not unusual, and in fact happens to everyone. Merely the circumstances and artifacts vary, as seen here surrounding you in the burnished silver, the porcelain and satin—slightly tarnished, minutely cracked, a tad worn. Nothing unusual at all. It can even be found on heater vents where rust forms in asymmetrical spots—something you routinely observe while feeling the presence of the person next door, as you and he stand quietly on either side of the metal partition, inhaling and exhaling.

Sleight of Fancy

I

WHEN SHE FIRST met him she did not care for the man: he smoked expensive, English cigarettes, and liked to speak French for sport.

Several months after she'd made his acquaintance, she was browsing in a used bookstore, looking at *Oeuvres*, a collection of writings by Arthur Cravan, speculating about whether or not it would come down in price, whether or not it would remain in the store until the following weekend. The man entered the bookstore, and so he wouldn't recognize her, she pulled her coat around her body, turned her back to the entrance. The man did not approach the French section, so she sat on a stool and continued to read.

He stood over her, and without speaking turned her hands so he could see what she was looking at. He began talking about Cravan—excitedly—about how interesting it was that no one knew exactly what had happened to him, how this had delayed Cravan's biography from being published. It would be considered bad scholarship to leave it that he disappeared in Mexico, probably robbed and beaten, and died in the desert—even though his body was never found.

People looked over at them, annoyed. The bookstore's clientele were serious readers—the place was always quiet and he was talking loudly. She became even angrier, replied that she knew who Cravan was in a tone of voice she hoped he would realize was a snub.

He took the book from her, began to read aloud in French.

She got up and left the store, livid that her afternoon in her favorite used bookstore had been ruined by an egocentric lout she barely knew. She was more angry still that she had been unassertive, that she was now walking in the rain on a Saturday afternoon with nothing to do and nowhere to go except back to her small studio apartment where she could hear the television of the man next door. To stay out would cost money. While she sat inside the bus stop enclosure, crowded because of the rain, she thought of Arthur Cravan, handsome poet and prize fighter—cohort and inspiration to the surrealists.

Come on, he said, and tugged at her arm. She pulled away and looked hopefully for the bus. He said he was sorry he had bothered her, and to please come with him now, let him buy her a cup of coffee to make it up to her. The bus wasn't coming.

They went into several cafés along the street, but went back out again because they wouldn't allow him to smoke. Finally they came to a place that had a smoking section and he bought her a cappuccino. He told her about himself: he'd been born in England. His mother was English, his father American. He'd been living in the city for two years. Without pausing he pulled a package from his backpack and placed *Oeuvres* on the table before her. It wasn't necessary for him to have done this, she could repay him, she said, thinking that actually she couldn't until that coming Friday. He said no, it was a good-will gift for having dis-

27

turbed her. She opened the book, he came around and sat next to her and they both looked through it, stopping at letters Cravan had written to Mina Loy—his wife, photographs of his boxing match with Jack Johnson, a drawing of Cravan in boxing togs done by Picabia. They studied several poems, pausing to do rough translations into English.

It was just getting dark when she put the book in her bag. They'd drunk several cappuccinos and were jittery. She expected him to invite her to his place, perhaps for dinner, perhaps not. She knew he would ask her to sleep with him. And she knew she would. Loneliness makes for poor judgment, she thought, makes for assigning attributes to people that they probably don't possess. She had condoms in her purse.

She noticed that although his place was dark and rather dingy, it was spruced up by many paintings and drawings.

Are you making love to me because of what you found me reading? she asked while he was inside and on top of her.

II

Soon after, she was living with the man. His apartment was in an interesting area of the city, a district where the sun broke through the fog and she could smell the sea. Immediately after she moved in, the man had a well-known photograph of Arthur Cravan enlarged to poster-size and added it to the collection on the wall.

Three months after moving in she was lonelier than ever, but without any solitude. When she came home from work he would be absorbed in whatever he was doing—reading, writing, watching a movie.

She caught him in several lies. He told her the art in the apartment had been done by students, friends. She found it odd it was all similar in style, yet the pictures bore several different signatures. While going through a closet to find some discarded clothing they used for cleaning rags, she'd come across a portfolio and looked through it. The sketches were signed by him and were stylistically the same as all the others.

Another time when she was angry with him, he'd slammed out the door and she began looking through his papers, saw on his passport that he had been born in New York, not England. She found other documents saying his mother had been English, but was deceased. He'd told her his mother lived in Cornwall.

Some people lie to embellish, to enhance others' opinions of them, but this man seemed to lie for pleasure.

III

The apartment's atmosphere became oppressive and gloomy. The problem was, she concluded, that driven by loneliness, she'd gone to live with him too soon. If she moved back into her own place, got some balance, things would be better between them.

She put in for extra hours at work, secretly opened a savings account to collect enough money to move.

The man came home one evening with a punching bag, some bolts and a jump rope. She told him he couldn't hang the bag because the bolts would make holes in the wall. He hung the bag anyway.

In the evenings when she arrived home from work and walked up the stairs to their apartment she could hear rhythmic sounds of the bag being struck. He'd stop when she walked in the door, sit at the table, have a glass of water, then return to the bag, or take up the rope and begin skipping. Sometimes she'd make herself something to eat and watch him exercise, sitting in the kitchen entry, balancing her food on her knees, while the man jumped and punched in the living room. She grew disturbed when it became apparent the man was obsessively in training for something.

IV

One evening the man was not exercising when she arrived. He came in an hour later holding a manuscript. He said he'd encountered someone who'd written a book in French. This person had offered him a good sum to translate it, and he already had the down payment; he threw five one-hundred dollar bills on the desk.

A friend discovered that he was translating professionally, and since the friend was starting a literary journal, he invited the man to contribute. The man enthusiastically began searching through *Oeuvres* for something suitable. After putting some of the poems into English, he asked the woman to look at what he'd done, to offer suggestions. Soon they were spending their weekends translating Cravan's work. They'd take books and a dictionary to a nearby café, a light place with many windows where the owners didn't care how long they stayed.

She felt closer to the man, and her mind felt lively, alive.

In the evenings the man sometimes went out—to confer with the person who'd hired him the put the book into English—he said. When he'd gone she opened the windows to clear the smoke, let fresh air into the apartment, and once out of boredom took a few swings at the bag. At first it flew back into her face, but she tried to remember what he had done, the rhythm he'd used, and after a month or so she became fairly good. She liked to pretend all her frustrations were flowing through her arms, out of her hands and into the bag. The more times she swung, the more she pushed them away. She imagined once that the bag was the man's face, but a sort of panic came over her and she swung tentatively, afraid.

V

The man said his work interested him so much that he no longer wanted to speak English—they would speak only in French. From that day on he spoke to her in the foreign language and she replied, thinking it was good practice, pleasurable as well. But when she forgot, or was too tired to use French he cut her off, or refused to answer.

They communicated in the foreign language so continually she believed it made them different people.

In order to work more effectively the man concluded he needed to lounge on their futon, use the reading lamp from the desk. He'd bought a bulb that was too strong a wattage for the lamp, screwed it in, and placed it over their bed. Every time she entered the room to get a book or sweater, he would glare at her, annoyed.

The man was becoming odder, more remote. When she allowed herself to think about it, she found that whatever infatuation she'd had for him had nearly dried up; his provocative green eyes were just green eyes; she didn't want him to touch her. Until, on occasion, he did.

She had almost saved enough money to move, and in order to keep out of the man's way she stayed in the kitchen in the evenings. Sometimes she would read, but she found she wasn't able to concentrate very well, and ended up playing solitaire. Solitaire afforded her the time to fantasize about what kind of apartment she would get, and in what district in the city, when she was able to get away. She looked forward to the evenings when the man would go out and she could punch the bag. She never told the man that she boxed and after her sessions, put her hands around the bag to still it, rearranged everything around the exercise space so he couldn't guess what she'd been doing.

On a Thursday evening she arrived home after the man had gone out. She found the first issue of the literary journal his friend had edited, saw in the table of contents that three of the Cravan translations were published and turned eagerly to the pages. He had not included her name on the translations. She threw the journal down, went to the punching bag, beat at it until she was quite sweaty and out of breath. When she had finished, her clothes were wet with perspiration. She sat in a chair drinking water, became chilled and went to shower.

She heard the man coming in and hurried to pull on her clothing, combed out her hair and took up her chair in the kitchen. The man wasn't translating. She shuffled the cards for a game of solitaire. He came into the kitchen, said he didn't feel like working and would she play cards with him. They played casino, blackjack, then hearts, which was not very enjoyable because it should be played by three or more people. After that she suggested a game she'd played in her adolescence—bloody knuckles. The loser is bashed on the knuckles by the winner, who uses the deck of cards as a weapon. The object was not to show any reaction to the pain. If the loser flinches the process is repeated. They played until both sets of knuckles on both their hands were cut, bloody and bruised, but they did not know who won because they had forgotten to keep score.

VI

The following day the woman came in and found all the art but the Cravan photograph ripped from the walls. She looked around—the apartment had been stripped. She circled the rooms, stunned. Eventually she came upon a note on the desk with her name on it. All it said was, "Went to Mexico." She sat in a chair looking at the three words. She thought maybe it was supposed to be funny.

She didn't know what to do, and so for a week she did nothing. During the second week she went to the movies several times to keep the emptiness in the apartment from making her agitated. On the weekend she called people she hadn't seen for quite a while.

The heaviness, the alienation she'd felt for so long began to lift.

She expected the man to return at any time, didn't know what she would do when he walked into the room. But he did not walk into the room.

She was free to go. She packed her things. He'd never put her name on the lease, or any of the bills. She merely wrote a check to him to cover her half of the expenses.

She would stay with a friend until she found a place. Her friend was happy to have her; she found it curious that when she lived with the man she'd unknowingly deteriorated to the extent that she hadn't had the energy to call anyone, to see anyone. Her isolation had grown so thick and dense that she'd only had the impetus to shuffle cards.

She packed her things, removed some items from the closet, and came across his portfolio of drawings. She assumed he'd forgotten it. She carried it to the center of the room, placed it among some other things he left behind, tossed *Oeuvres* onto the pile.

When she was finished packing she dead-bolted the door, went down the stairs and threw her set of keys through the nearly closed window.

VII

In a month's time she'd gotten an apartment, and in several more months a sense of self back. During the interim she'd made the acquaintance of another man. When he spoke, she was usually able to guess what he'd say before he said it, and he pestered her for sex the way children pester their parents for toys. He was stable, usually affable, and never became particularly anxious or upset. When this present man made love to her she needed to pretend it was the other—and this surprised her because she had been sure she felt nothing for her former lover.

Early one morning she woke from dreaming of the other, saw the present man snoring lightly next to her and slapped him across the face; he often attributed her behavior to something amiss with her hormones.

VIII

A year later she was more deeply entrenched with the present man. When he was moving about inside her, eyes closed in some private pleasure, she believed she hated him. She found his obliviousness to her feelings fascinating; he could never know her well, a fact which made her feel protected, cozy.

She began, again, to play cards using the same deck she had with her former lover, running her hands over the smooth, brightly colored surfaces. Once, after an argument, she tried to coax the present man into a game of bloody knuckles, but he proved such a poor card player that she took pity after she bashed his left hand and abandoned the game.

On Saturday afternoons she resumed visiting her favorite bookstore, taking refuge in books. How had it come about that her life had turned out so oddly? Yet her friends would not conclude the same: she had a steady job, a devoted partner, friends, a life—is how they saw it. Her.

In the French section, she looked through various titles, came, again, across *Oeuvres*, wondered if it was her former copy. Someone had tried to remove the notations she and the man made in the margins, but they were still visible. Red flecks from an eraser fell from the pages. Although the price had gone up, she decided she must have it.

She took *Oeuvres* to the cafe where she and the man had first gone. On the way there she passed the bus stop. A bus was coming and she suddenly had the urge to run out in front of it, but stood motionless in the street until the impulse had passed. In the café she looked through *Oeuvres,* remembering who had translated what, the arguments they'd had about which way to render certain lines, Cravan's legend.

In the weeks that followed, she vowed to put her former lover out of her mind.

Soon she was unable to conjure the image of the other, didn't dream of him at all; it was as if that place in her mind where she held him had been erased.

A postcard arrived from Mexico a month later, postmarked at the time she had begun to forget him. The front was hand-done, a collage of Cravan, with the line "La vie est atroce," visible through the image. On the back it read, "Gone for good."

She stepped out of doors to catch the bus to go to her job, looked around, and wondered when had the world become so monochromatic?

Inklings

MORPHING

There is an ovum. A sperm fertilizes it. There is an embryo that becomes a fetus. It gestates for nine months and enters the world. When it is placed in its crib, the parents and other relatives peer at it.

It is one. It is two. It is a girl in a lace dress at Christmas dinner, crying and hanging onto her mother's velvet gown during the family photo.

There is trouble in kindergarten, she does not want to play house, pretends to set it on fire, which upsets the other little girls; she does not want to take naps or eat Graham Crackers. There are eccentrics on both sides. Her parents glare at each other, each thinking the others' family peculiarities are the more severe and problematic.

Then everyone relaxes because the girl now looks like her mother. *Pretty, pretty,* people exclaim, both family and strangers. Since that is the case, it doesn't really matter what she does. She punches a boy on the playground and he does not hit her back, she can ignore her homework and only get a reprimand. She is so cute.

During adolescence she grows, she changes. She no longer looks like her mother. Who is this person? They scrutinize her. Ah, she is beginning to look like Bill's side of the family. *What a shame* the relatives cry, and secretly fear a need for rhinoplasty.

Almost overnight she has gone from being one of the most popular girls to a tall, lonely teen. *As least she is tall* people say. *Great tits* others comment.

The tall girl with her large breasts takes up basketball and joins the team. Here, she forges another identity for herself. Her family goes to her games and they cheer. *But who is athletic* they ask each other?

In college the girl settles into her features and once again looks like her mother. "A beautiful woman" is how she is seen, and it startles her, for she has forgotten what it was like to be cultivated for her appearance.

When she walks down the street she often sees her reflection in windows—what she perceives as herself, her essence and being, never seems to be inside the image in the glass. This form, on which approval was bestowed, that lost it, and receives it again, is like being inside a living, breathing vertical chalk line, that shape made during homicide investigations, and this outline is the only thing that separates her from the world.

She isn't particularly concerned about the countenance she projects— and never was—but she knows she will be monitored by her family for the next ten years or twenty, until they grow too old to care, or are too preoccupied with their health to take an interest. She will continue to morph, first resembling one side of the family and then the other, changing in tiny, infinitesimal ways—while she walks and talks, while she eats, sleeps, has sex and ages, propelled along by the pull of gravity, the push of genetics.

What? What did he say? The actor has just uttered a line. She whispers in his ear. When she is finished, those around them are once again able to concentrate on the screen.

What was that? he bellows. She again leans over and mumbles something, undoubtedly filling him in on the dialogue he is unable to hear. The audio is loud, almost too loud; the man must suffer from extensive hearing loss to be unable to discern it. *Huh? Shut up* someone in the audience shouts. *Shhh,* his wife reiterates.

There are several ways of thinking about this: one is that this poor old man in his declining years cannot even enjoy a movie any longer. The other is that this individual was probably a self-centered lout since he was young—not caring who he disturbed in public places. Or perhaps there is a history of extreme frugality and he will not pay for a hearing device.

The man in the movie is a suave character who lies and cheats and has sex with lots of women, an antihero the audience is supposed to like.

The antihero is having more sex. It is graphic, with moaning. The old man doesn't need this interpreted for him. He is quiet. Does he still get erections? Does his wife wish he didn't?

Toward the end of the film it looks like the antihero will get his comeuppance, a Hollywood ending that disappoints. The law has set a trap for him which he will undoubtedly fall for. There has been foreshadowing. *Why did he do that?* the man yells. A group of four young men sitting in front of him turn as if they rehearsed it and scream *Dammit, shut up!* They might be college boys, or the dark could make them appear younger.

Ouch, the man hollers as his wife climbs over him, treading on his foot. She is moving down the aisle, she is opening the door, throwing a long rectangle of light onto the back rows, a line of patrons squinting in the sudden brightness. The door falls shut again. The ensuing silence makes it seem like a different movie.

Someone enters the theatre. The man looks up but the figure keeps moving, sits down in one of the front rows. It could be someone who has arrived early for the next screening.

The final song on the soundtrack is playing and credits drift down the screen. People are beginning to gather their things and head to the exit. Some of the lights go up, and those further down the row climb over the man who is still in his seat, shouting *Linnea! Linnea! Linnea!*

WARPING

She dyes her hair blonde, takes up the hems of her skirts and what follows is a husband. Her husband is a man who likes blonde hair and short skirts—he encourages her to keep bleaching, and to work on those hems. A year or so into their marriage, the man informs her he has a way with women. The woman is fairly certain he does not have a way with her, for she often regrets having married him. Naturally he had not informed her of his ex-wives who threw him out, or his former girlfriends who'd changed their phone numbers and threatened to get restraining orders.

While they are out in public, the man will see a young woman in a vehicle decreasing her speed, or circling the block, and will say, *See that young woman over there, she wants me. There is a definite attraction.* The young woman in question—and many others—will often give up trying to park on the street, and put their cars in a nearby garage, afterwards obliviously passing the couple on the sidewalk. *Well, she sees I am with you,* is how he explains it.

As the marriage continues, the man comes to believe his fictions. He is a lady-killer and his wife is lucky he stays around. To solidify his advantage, he threatens her with the affairs he might have any moment. Over time his stories begin to consume the day-to-day reality, and the man's fictions become his wife's as well.

Many years later the woman still bleaches what is left of her hair, and wears short skirts. She continues to attract attention, but more in the manner of confusion and shock. She trails after her husband, suspicious he is having illicit affairs with beautiful women in their twenties. The man adjusts his support hose and says that although young women still desire him, are quite admiring and willing, he's put that sort of thing on hold for a time, and does she want to accompany him to the bank so he can deposit his pension check? She takes his arm and they slowly make their way down First Avenue. He occasionally stops to lean against a building to rest. As he does so, she keeps her eye out for young women on the street who might be trying to seduce him. When they pass plate glass, they straighten their posture and hold up their heads, for seeing their reflections makes them quietly hope they are important.

IMPLODING

He has a chance to be one of the best ever, has the correct body type and the talent. Unlike most, he performs better before a large stadium crowd. He has begun to win medals and receive notoriety—photographs of him, arms open, breaking the tape— or on a podium holding a medal are frequently in the papers.

He begins skipping practices, starts to drink scotch and eat fattening food. *There is nothing I love anymore.*

Get it together his coach shouts. *Think of all the years we've spent. . . .*

But the man is too close to the years, cannot differentiate them from the present and no longer knows what they mean. By the season's end he has lost three major competitions and does not make the world team. His coach drops him.

When he is older, he gets up morning after morning to teach what he used to do so consummately, so sublimely—to youths who will never achieve the same. Occasionally after practice a parent of one of the children he coaches musters the courage to shyly ask him what happened, and will look away. *Our world is so insular* he says, indicating the track. *It forces us to turn in on ourselves. No place to go.*

RECEDING

(A WELL-TRAVELED PATH)

Today the young woman is to meet with her writing professor.
She has worked on her stories for several weeks, has read them
aloud to herself and showed them to her peers, trying to make
them as polished as possible before the tutorial. She changes the
cartridge of her printer and prints out clear, dark copies so they
will be easy to read, puts the stories in her book bag and hurries
to the cafe. Her writing professor said he would prefer to meet in
a place that plays opera and serves wine, telling her it relaxes him
and will make him a better judge of her work. She wishes the
sessions could continue to take place on campus, since she gets
together with her friends afterwards in the student lounge, but
she is proud he has taken an interest in her writing and agrees to
the cafe conference.

The professor is waiting when she arrives, a carafe and two
glasses on the table. The woman doesn't really want any wine, as
drinking it in the afternoon gives her a headache, but she sup-
poses she should take a little to be polite. He asks for her stories,
and suggests they order some food, handing her a menu. He
quickly glances over her work, not taking the trouble to remove
his pen from his shirt pocket to write any comments, looks up
and says *not bad*, saving his compliments for her eyes and hair-
style.

He asks her what bands she likes, mentions several names in
alternative rock, so she will think him contemporary and peer-

like. He pays the check and suggests they meet again in two weeks, same time, same place.

While driving back to campus the young woman is almost in tears, is angry and humiliated. Why won't the writing professor take her work seriously? Is it because she wears decent clothes and has her hair professionally cut? If she wore ripped jeans and shaved her head would he at least make suggestions in the margins?

Maybe she should see the department head and try and study with someone else, but she would have to get special permission to do that and what could she say to receive it, save tell the truth? She knows that if she goes to the dean, the professor will retaliate. She'll be branded a troublemaker in a mostly male department.

At the edges of her anger, she is embarrassed and uncomfortable. The professor has forgotten how fatuous and strange people appear when they try to behave in a youthful manner, after passing from youth so long ago.

She remembers reading about how women were once supposed to feel flattered, privileged when singled out as sex objects by men with power, but as the earth rotated and time receded, the professor rejected the concept of feminism, the use of computers and other facts of everyday existence, and began to cling to a ghost reality—or has the world hurled forward without him noticing?

Before taking the turn that leads to campus, the young woman passes a pawn shop, and slams on her brakes to look for a parking place. She shall buy herself a hocked engagement ring, and the next time she sees the professor will tell him she has become engaged to her boyfriend. To follow his line of thinking, he will then see her as a claim already staked out by another man—there being a male involved will suffice, she thinks, to keep him at bay.

She finds a gold ring with a little diamond, which the proprietor will sell her for fifty dollars, and pays with her credit card, chalking it up to yet another school expense.

CAREENING

It was once a country lane, is now a well-traveled road, a short cut for commuters to access the freeway. The area remains an enclave of countryside, surrounded by suburbs.

Animals flock here, their original habitats destroyed by the sprawl. The red-winged blackbird makes its nest in hayfields. Raccoons, possums and other indigenous creatures arrive, as do feral cats.

Some of the cats are cultivated by those who live in the area. Country-dwellers buy cans of cat food and leave them in backyards—in the shade of large trees, or on patios. The kittens may tentatively bond with those predisposed to liking the cats, but this bond is tenuous—a sudden move by the cat fancier could irrevocably spook the animal. The adult felines hiss and spit, their striped faces contorted with dislike and distrust.

Encouraged by the young cats' response, the country-dwellers purchase cat brushes and small rubber balls. The animals stare at the brushes or shiny silver combs and slink away under bushes, or will watch, puzzled, as the balls roll over ground-cover into clusters of weeds.

Although these animals do not make satisfactory pets, people wandering about their homes in between tasks will watch them from windows or from behind bushes in their gardens, fascinated by the cats handsomeness, their lustrous coats, glinting green eyes and nonchalant grace.

Most of the animals living in the country are compelled to explore other fields and pastures, which often leads to their crossing the road. At the beginning of any given day, when fog encloses the area like a gray umbrella, there could be a random string of carcasses lying over the five-mile stretch.

Every morning the country dwellers come out of their houses in pajamas or bathrobes, their bodies still weighted with sleep, and slowly walk down long driveways to the morning paper, keeping their eyes fixed on the gravel. At the driveway's end, anxiety tightens their chests and breathing is difficult. With silent supplication they take deep breaths, hoping the expanse of road before them will be free of lifeless bodies when they finally, and with apprehension, raise their eyes. As fog veils their faces and hands they know it has come to affect them more than they ever imagined, these misty morning confrontations.

She watches as they blow out all the votive candles, climb statues of St. Joseph and the Virgin Mary. When they jump to the floor they are flushed and excited. *What else?* The boy's friend thinks they should take their clothes off and run up and down the aisles naked. Too risky, they decide. *I know,* the altar boy sprints to the altar. The key is in the tabernacle. He turns it, reaches his hand inside, takes a package of communion wafers and rips it open. His little sister gasps from one of the pews. Her brother and his friend stuff some into their mouths and pronouncedly chew. After swallowing they rush over to the pew and the girl's brother thrusts some wafers to her lips. She turns her head away and refuses to open her mouth, but he presses her jawbones with both hands, forces her mouth open and shoves one in before she is able to push him away. *It's probably a sin to spit it out, blessed or not* he gloats. The boys munch on the communion wafers like they are cookies, but the girl swallows reluctantly, ashamed she isn't letting it dissolve on her tongue as she was taught to do.

When they finish the packet the boys scan the church. Pounding on the organ might attract the attention of the priest, or the cleaning lady. Her brother walks to the altar and stops to think. He tries a door behind the altar that the priest enters through every Sunday. It opens.

Try and find the wine his friend mutters. They search, but the cabinets are locked. There is a row of priest's cassocks hung on a portable rack. The altar boy grabs his sister. *Put this on.* The boys put the cassock over her clothes and button it up. The sleeves hang down past her knees, and the gown spills out over the floor. Her brother spreads his legs and indicates she should get down on her hands and knees and crawl through them. *Do it or we'll say* YOU *stole the communion wafers. You know they'll believe me.* As she is crawling he spanks her. His friend stands a foot behind him and does the same. *More!* The girl turns around and crawls back through their legs while they continue slapping her. The cassock drags across the floor, collecting dust, becomes entangled in the boys' feet and legs. *Crawl, crawl* the boys shout excitedly as their adrenaline flows and they spank harder.

° ° °

The girl who teaches their catechism class has knobby knees that jut out above her knee socks, and likes to talk about the hairshirts of St. Elizabeth.

She is frightened of her young students, and everyone knows that mayhem could erupt at any moment, or the children could simply rise, go outdoors and play, as they once did, leaving the startled student-teacher open-mouthed, standing before a blackboard, alone in an empty room. It is only the threat of the parish priest bursting in and yelling *test* that keeps the children in check. When he enters and cries *test*, the class is supposed to take a blank piece of paper and write down responses to questions he fires at them, such as, "What is the judgment called which will be passed on each one of us immediately after death?" "Why do we honor relics?" or, "Is the Holy Ghost a dove?" The little girl knows her catechism well and continually receives the priest's *well done*—while just as continually, a boy three seats down who does not bother to write anything, is swatted alongside the head with his catechism book by the now irate and enraged padre.

On Easter Sunday the priest is uttering: "Do you not know that a little yeast has its effect all through the dough? Get rid of the old yeast to make yourselves fresh dough, unleavened loaves, as it were; Christ our Passover has been sacrificed. Let us celebrate the feast not with the old yeast, that of corruption and wickedness, but with the unleavened bread of sincerity and truth." The little girl grows dizzy, faints and has to spend the rest of the mass outdoors on the front steps of the church, hunched over, her head on her knees. Her concerned father comes out now and again to check on her. When the mass is over, the family rejoins the girl and they solemnly shuffle to the parking lot.

They hope the little girl is not so ill as to cause them to miss brunch.

As they drive to the restaurant, her altar boy brother sullenly leans over and mumbles: *you always did have to be the center of attention.*

o o o

When in her early 20s the young woman visits New York City for the first time, and while walking down Fifth Avenue she sees a cathedral, guesses it to be St. Patrick's. She is hesitant about whether or not to enter, not having been inside a church since she was approaching adolescence, when her parents decided The Church's views on birth control and divorce were out of touch with the contemporary world, and none of them needed attend any longer.

St. Patrick's, though, is also a famous tourist attraction, and many of its stained glass windows were made in Chartes. She goes up the stairs. In the nave there are many tourists milling about, and signs saying "No Flash Photography." Further inside, the architecture and dimensions of the church are intimidating. The scent of votive candle wax, and that church smell of mustiness and time, is causing her stomach to tighten, her body to tense. She finds herself reflexively placing her hand in holy water and shocked, pulls it back out. The candles make spitting sounds as they splutter and burn. While she stands next to a pew she finds her knees bending in genuflection, hangs onto the thick, brown wood to stay upright. The altar is a long way off. Interspersed among the pews are those with heads bent in prayer, unselfconscious and remote in their intensity. She is embarrassed, as if catching them in an extremely private act. As she grips the pew, she is staggered that something as innocuous as walking into a place of stones, stained glass and spires is flinging her back to the state of being too little and terrified, and no one even notices how she is being reeled back into the past, delivered there by sensory receptors and somatic senses, psyche and flesh.

Tell me what you see. His head is in a contraption, a lens several inches from his eye. He notes some letters, black against a white background in a sans serif type, probably Helvetica, but that is not what he says.

He is asked to read smaller and smaller rows of letters until he is no longer able to distinguish them, after which the doctor makes notes on a sheet of paper, moves the contraption to the other side of his face and puts a lens to his other eye. If there are still letters showing it is not apparent, and the physician becomes annoyed, as if the man is not trying. But he sees only some black lines, blurred grays, a landscape of abstraction. As he attempts to focus, staring intently into the strange vista, his is able to discern a very tall mountain range, a woman weeping at the bottom, her tears minuscule black dots moving down her face. Perhaps the woman weeps because unlike the alps, her time on earth is minimal, her being in relation to such geology insignificant.

The physician exchanges the lens for several others until the scene becomes obscured and letters stand in a line before the man, dark and brightly delineated.

Indebted

A DISTRESSED MAN studies his phone bill which has risen by fifty percent. The same number is listed over and over again and he recognizes it as belonging to a woman who lives in another part of the state. She is young, single, with a child to support, is in the business he was in before he retired, and frequently calls to ask his advice. She telephones early in the morning, during the dinner hour and on holidays. If the man is present he will jump up and take her call, much to the annoyance of his family. When he returns home he rushes to play his messages and promptly get back to her—which has resulted in the exorbitant increase in his bill. The woman does not heed the advice the man gives her, in fact she often does just the opposite. Nonetheless, the man thinks this communication a necessary and worthwhile expenditure, despite having to write a check for 1/4 of his pension to the telephone company.

When the man comes home one day, he goes to his answering machine and there are no messages. For the next several days the phone does not ring. When he picks it up one morning to make a call, he discovers there is no dial tone. He tells his wife that he is going to the neighbor's house to report that their telephone is out of order, but she tells him not to bother, she had it disconnected; they simply cannot afford his behavior any longer. She picks up the book she was reading.

The following morning the man wonders what to do with himself. He can tell that after all the years of going to work, his presence in the house hour after hour puts his wife on edge. He thinks he will walk to a newsstand, purchase the local paper and read the section that lists "volunteers wanted" while sitting in the park. The only people on the benches are old age pensioners like himself, and women with small children. When he pauses to watch the children in the playground, imbued with such energy and high spirits, their mothers or nannies glare, sit upright and become ultra-vigilant.

The man is disappointed to find that the volunteer positions are all dull or depressing—helping out with holiday crafts fairs, dressing in a Santa Claus outfit and ringing a bell while standing next to a large iron pot, or going into nursing homes and reading to senior citizens. The thought of reading to sedated elderly people only slightly older than himself who are too medicated to understand anything he says, is chilling.

A pack of dogs straining on their leashes enters the park from the south side, a young man in tow. The man lurches after them and frequently looks at his watch. A minute or so later the group reaches the middle of the park where one of the dogs stops to defecate. The young man takes the opportunity to light a cigarette. Twenty-five yards further another dog does the same, while minutes later still another lifts its leg on the base of a water fountain. The older man is outraged, strides over to the dogs' caretaker and splutters: *How could you not clean up after those ani-*

mals? Children run and play in the area. You are a party to spreading disease and filth! The young man shrugs his shoulders and races off, the dogs leading the way. The man walks back to where he was sitting. He knows the young man thought him a meddler who has nothing better to do than try and police other people, a man whose life is so devoid of anything that he becomes upset over dog shit. Nonetheless, the man takes comfort in knowing he is in the right and the young man is wrong—careless and negligent.

The man spends the next several days in the park, and his wife shows her appreciation by cooking nice suppers upon his return. He is appalled to discover that the young man is not the only irresponsible park-goer—most of the people with dogs are more like the young man than not. This at first irks the man, then makes him furious. Over the weekend he charges up to several dog owners demanding they clean up their animal's mess. Some pretend he isn't there, and stare over his head at the treetops; others tell him to fuck off, and still others narrow their eyes, grinning while their dogs menacingly bare their teeth at him. Whenever these incidents occur, a park attendant never seems to be on duty, and an attempt to report these occurrences to the washroom janitors proves futile when he discovers none of the janitors speak English.

One Monday he passes a drug store and sees they are having a sale on various items, most of them useless this time of year. Near a row of checkstands he notices some children's things, a plastic wading pool, several beach balls, some small buckets and shovels for making sand castles. He purchases the latter items.

Unbeknownst to the man, he is frequently observed. The sight of him in late autumn, in his black pants and overcoat charging after dogs, a bright blue shovel in one hand, a blue bucket decorated with pink starfish and shells in the other, is the source of amusement or alarm, depending a park-goer's point of view. One woman who thought he was approaching to mug her, shrieked and called the police after she'd set her dog on him and the animal ran the other way. The dispatcher did not bother to send any law enforcement, explaining that no crime was being committed.

By early winter the man is a fixture in the park, and some, especially those who come on weekends to walk or jog, hand him tips. At first the man is confused by people trying to give him money, but is soon grateful and happy to accept it. When he has enough, he thinks, he will get a money order, possibly take it to the utility company and purchase a secret telephone number and voice mail, then go to the post office and rent a post office box for the bill, or will perhaps save enough to take a vacation alone, in a place with a warm climate, wide beaches, where animals are permitted.

Spring

HE TOUCHES HER face and leans forward to kiss her. Her breasts press into him, his tongue is deep in her mouth. The man suddenly opens his eyes, pulls away and takes several steps back. He walks into the converted chicken house where he lives and slams the door.

She follows him but he has locked her out. Standing on her tiptoes she can see him through the window and smell the kerosene lamp he's just lit. His back is to her and he is at the table, again bent over his books. She sits on the grass, wondering what to do. It will be dark soon. She waits fifteen minutes, but he does not reappear. The woman pulls her keys from her purse and walks to her car. She will drive the half an hour back to town, back to the tiny house she rented when the man came to her one day and told her he was moving out—to a one-room cabin without electricity on a large farm in the country. She thought it would just be temporary, that he would get tired of it. Instead he became a vegetarian and said: 'Devotion is from the Latin word to vow, meaning to yield, to commit, to consecrate oneself to the object of devotion, without regard to the sacrifice involved.'

She passes the farms and pastures lying on either side of the two-lane road. It does not surprise her, really, that the man should be doing this—he is the son of an investment banker, played on the tennis team of his private high school, and summered on Martha's Vineyard. Most of his adult life has been spent escaping his upbringing—like many men who came of age in a certain era.

His transformation came on gradually—the sex seemed obligatory and then it disappeared entirely—but he said nothing was wrong. She spent time jumping on and off the scale to see if she'd gained weight, and looking into mirrors, at her thighs for cellulite, at her head for gray hair.

She didn't think it strange when he read the Bible, or Augustine or St. John of the Cross, for the two of them read quite widely and this type of inquiry did not seem odd.

She can see the lights of the town just beginning to stand out in the twilight as she follows the road that descends from the hills. She hopes the woman with whom she shares the little house will have gone out, or if she is there, she will be in her room and will not come out to talk. When she gets home she sits on her bed and sighs.

After ten years together, five of them as man and wife, they are supposed to be friends. She often thinks that if they'd had a family none of this would have happened, but they wanted it to be just the two of them.

Several months ago when she'd driven out for a visit, as she always did because he didn't have transportation, she stopped in the middle of the road and watched him in front of his chicken house, dancing, leaping, throwing his arms about. She'd never seen anyone but children and animals that happy. She turned around near a cattle crossing and drove back home.

He attempted to explain it to her—how it feels when he is one with The Lord—the joy, the ease with which he walks in the world, and how content he is in his body, but not really *in* his body. . .he tried to avoid clichés, use odd analogies—like sports or dance—how, if you were giving a physical performance and all that you'd practiced had come together at just that instant—there is no struggle, no pain, and the euphoria, how the mind soars—it is almost unbearable, like watching the sun. Once you experience this, he says, there is no going back, and every time he touches her, loves her, he can't find the Lord for days. And when he is lost from Him it is as if he is dying, not leaving his body, happily, as if his earthly time is over, just annihilated. He cannot live without the sustenance he receives from that communion. It is not fair of her to ask him to.

Thursday: the day she goes out to his cabin. She packs up some food—canned goods, tomatoes and oranges. He is thinner each time they meet. They will sit and visit at the rotting picnic table next to his house. She will not try to touch him. He will not invite her in.

She hides her resentment, her confusion and behaves as his friend. He is happy to see her.

Her cheek is tingling. She is sure he left a red mark. He gets up from the picnic table and glowers. What did she say? A quip? Something slightly sarcastic? He misunderstood, whatever it was. Or something slipped out, some words, unconsciously. He strides to the chicken house, locks the door behind him and shouts from the window: *no one on this earth, or in this life has the right to be jealous of God.*

Respite

A MAN REMOVES his clothes and stands naked in a dim room. He looks at his thin arms, his skinny legs, remembers when his body pulsed with vitality, tries not to think about it.

Several minutes later a woman enters. She remains clothed and seats herself in a chair. The man goes toward her, climbs onto her lap, draws his legs to his chest and presses his face into her neck. He cries, soon cries harder. Neither of them speaks, but the woman holds him, occasionally stroking his narrow shoulders, his frail back. When the man is finished he gets up, wipes his eyes, goes to his pants and pulls out her payment, as he did the week before, the week before that, and as he will do again.

Sleep

CATS' SLEEP IS a lot like ours. Both humans and felines sleep lying down, both frequently make twitching movements while in the REM phase, and it is interesting to note that many cats snore. We believe cats also dream much in the way we do, dream of chasing, or of being chased—although what pursues and flees is often different for them. They may dream of being one step ahead of large, ugly dogs, while we dream of running from angry men wielding knives. Or, in turn, they could have lovely, slow-motion dreams of pouncing on a hapless gopher or mouse, while we dream of triumphantly punching a significant other in the stomach.

A particular woman is rather catlike, preferring solitude to company, opting for independence rather than acquiescence, and when frightened or startled she frequently lashes out.

While sleeping, she often dreams the usual dreams of flight, pursuit, or falling, noting that in the falling dreams she somehow always manages to land on her feet.

Upon awakening the woman does not always know what transpired in her dreams. When she sits up, she sees the cat sprawled at the foot of the bed and remembers that during the night it had settled on the other pillow where she dreamed it was a teddy bear, placed in the bed for comfort and support. She recalls that during part of the dream the bear turned into a doll—first a harlequin, then a Pinocchio—its nose is not what grew longer, and finally a marionette, bobbing and turning, without evidence of a puppeteer's hands, or wires, or string.

The woman leans back against the headboard and remembers a tale she once heard, or perhaps read—puppets always seek their puppeteers to imbue them with life, and once this is accomplished, they never have to touch back down on earth again. The puppeteer, however, desires the puppet's state—its natural grace and lack of consciousness, and the human condition lies somewhere between that of a puppet and a god.

The woman gets out of bed, and the cat, awakened by her movements, leaps to the floor. As the woman puts on her dressing gown she looks around the room, becomes aware that it feels smaller this morning, the walls seem closer and much too white.

The cat runs down the hallway, ahead of the woman, knowing it is to be let out. As she unlocks the French door it darts into the yard, spies a bird sitting in a rosemary bush. It flattens its ears, crouches, stalks the bird, and pounces. The bird flies into a nearby oak tree, alighting on a thin branch jutting from the foliage. The woman softly closes the door and through the small glass panes sees the cat open its mouth, hears the faint sounds it makes in its effort to charm the bird. The bird, of course, does not respond; the cat slinks along the ground and begins climbing the tree. The woman turns and makes her way down the hallway, aware of the floor's coldness. As she moves she feels her feet making contact with the polished wood, how the toes grasp and release. She needs to do something, and flings her hand out to her side. She throws out her other hand, flings the first arm over-head, then the other. Grasping both arms behind her, she locks her fingers and arches into a backbend, snaps forward, spins in concentric circles, then jumps up and down. Yet in spite of these gyrations the woman is unable to free herself from her somno-lence.

The cat, also thwarted, sits in the crotch of the tree licking its paws as it surveys the yard for a secluded place to resume sleeping in the early-morning sun.

Visitations

AFTER NOT HAVING seen it for a time they are always startled by how nice it looks, surprised it hasn't fallen into disrepair because that is what they remember, sadness and disintegration—or think they remember. But its whiteness gleams, its stained glass glows in primary colors, the porch is devoid of webs and dirt, and the lounge chairs are newish, clean.

Just for a moment, on the porch ringing the bell, or fumbling with the key, the idea crosses their minds that they might be wrong, might have remembered wrong. But after they let themselves in, or are greeted at the door and step inside, the heaviness descends and grows increasingly pronounced as they pass through the rooms.

They look around at the familiar furniture, always noting how much bigger it looked when they were small, realize the reaction is a common one.

They exchange pleasantries with their parents, who are sometimes in the midst of their routines when they arrive—gardening, listening to the radio, or watching television. Their parents stop what they are doing, attempting to hide their annoyance at being interrupted, trying not to show their displeasure that time has gotten away from them and nothing is ready.

When refreshment is prepared, always by their mother, they usually have it in the house, although the children politely suggest taking it in the backyard or front porch to escape the house's interior. But their mother often feels a chill, doesn't like the idea that an insect might hover or crawl while they are having a snack.

Inside, around the dining table or living room the children try and fight the melancholy that oppresses them as they sit in the chairs from so long ago. The chairs have, of course, been refurbished since then. Sometimes the subject of present or future refurbishings takes up a good portion of the conversation, and when this occurs everyone feels less tense. If the children have brought their own children, they invariably grow quiet, sometimes afraid; they feel an inarticulated anxiousness that manifests itself as being nervous about spilling something on grandma's couch or table, or by grabbing their parent's arm and saying, *I want to go home.*

The children often talk in loud voices about their careers or their spouses or what their children are up to in order to rally against the atmosphere. During these segments of the conversation they are often surprised by their parents' responses—how, as time passed, two liberals have grown conservative. They've noticed their father as of late has had difficulty following the interaction, that over the past several visits he's had a hard time comprehending what was said—a fact they tell to their spouses, but not their own mother or siblings, for it seems a matter of less importance if not spoken of to them.

Their mother, who looks as if she'd rather be in her garden, tries to hide a sigh, also her fear that her grandchildren will damage one of her possessions.

A bright moment usually occurs when the parents take their children and grandchildren out of doors to show them the improvements they've made in the yard, or a new bush in bloom. The children spring up eagerly; their own children race out of the house where they jump and shout in relief.

After looking at the changes in the yard, the visit is usually, by unspoken agreement, over. Occasionally there is perfunctory talk of the children and grandchildren staying to dinner, but all know this is just a gesture. Their mother despises cooking, would not want her son or daughters messing about in her kitchen, and their parents, particularly their mother, does not like to go out. It costs a great deal of money to eat out, they tell their children, frowning slightly to convey they do not approve of them wasting money on such things.

That their parents must live austerely because they are elderly and afraid is implied—even though they are free of debt and have plenty of money. The children have discussed this among themselves over the telephone. One of the daughters informed the others it is called Depression-Era Syndrome.

When all the kissing is over the children try not to hurry to their cars. After the final waves they accelerate slowly to give the impression they have just had a pleasurable experience.

As they round the corner to get on the street that takes them to the freeway, they feel their sadness, their despondency, beginning to lift. Their own children are unusually silent, sullen, after these visits and they feel a rush of guilt for having taken them there—consider telling their parents that the kids are involved in so many activities they will only be able to bring them over on Thanksgiving and Christmas.

The further away from their parents' house they get, the more they feel like the picture they have of themselves—enthusiastic and basically happy people who have loving and pleasant parents. They sigh, grateful for the open spaces lying on either side of the freeway. While searching for cheerful, uncomplicated music to listen to on their cassette players or car radios, they speculate yet again about what it could be in that bright Victorian structure that can make them feel so terrible, so lifeless after all these years. Yet all they recall are elusive impressions—the way the sunlight played through the upstairs French window illuminating a square of hardwood floor, or the dark hallways, or an even blurrier memory—of themselves, or a sibling, crying in the living room window seat, head pressed against the glass and wishing to get out.

Prescriptions

WE BELIEVE THERE might be something wrong with us or that we have gone crazy. We clandestinely write pop screenplays hoping to someday become famous directors of blockbusters, simultaneously study difficult tracts on postmodern culture. We imagine being married, and at the same time insist we do not enjoy the company of men and fantasize about a same-sex experience. Of course we wish to remain married though we spend most of our spare time pursuing single women. We continually dream of shedding weight while we eat an entire medium pizza at one sitting. We believe we show the world how mature and responsible we are, but while driving in our cars with the windows rolled tightly we blast music with lyrics of adolescent angst and feel empathy. We enjoy the comfort of stuffed animals, but when friends come to visit hide them away, or if we forget to do this, say they belong to nieces and nephews. We think we believe in things, have convictions and opinions, but cannot always be certain of what they are. We often feel stupid—or wildly intelligent. We suspect we are disintegrating so we redouble our efforts to appear stable and competent.

Today is Monday. We put one foot in front of the other, raise our coffee mugs to our lips. Tick the clock goes. That word has always made us nervous. We know we have names, identities, personas, but we're confused and can't recall what they are. To muster courage we remind ourselves to follow our narratives, those horizontal lines supposed to lead somewhere.

Circa

THE GIRL RETURNS home from school, passes through the garden gate and finds her father urinating onto some bushes in the backyard. She closes the latch softly, walks as quietly as she can. Once inside the house she looks through the sliding glass door; his back is to her and he is dressed in his gardening attire—blue jeans and a sweatshirt. She somehow senses that he is aware of her presence. Her father finishes peeing, zips up his fly and continues his work, inspects a cluster of rosebushes, and then stares at a limb of an oak tree. The girl has a strange feeling in her stomach as she walks to her room to change out of her school clothes, a feeling she tries to dismiss when she sits at the kitchen table picking at her afternoon snack.

Midway through summer the girl, bored, begins playing handball against the garage door after dinner. She is not particularly good and the ball sometimes gets away from her. Once when she runs to retrieve it, she again comes upon her father relieving himself on some bushes by the side of the house. She stands clutching the ball, her stomach tight. The girl believes he is again aware of her, although he does not shift his gaze from the wooden slats of the house. She tiptoes back to the garage door and tells herself to think of nothing but keeping the ball going, of slamming it into the wood.

A week or so later the girl searches through the garage for her hula hoop and discovers her father's beer, several brown bottles, hidden in various nooks. Two of the bottles are completely covered with dust, as if he has forgotten them, but on a lower shelf is a clean bottle, probably placed there recently. The girl understands why he has hidden the bottles, as she, too, has faced the consequences of doing something of which her mother does not approve. She has overheard her mother's sarcasm vented on her father from various parts of the house when he did something that displeased her, so she does not remove the bottles and fling them into the dumpster down the street.

Both the girl and her father spend a lot of time outdoors because this is what her mother seems to prefer. If the girl and her father remain in the house too long after supper, her mother sighs, grows irritable, and either the girl or her father will be the first to drift outside, she to hit the ball against the garage door, and her father to meander in the garden, carrying a hedge clipper or rake.

On some evenings when she does not want to play ball, she sits with her legs crossed under a large willow tree drawing pictures of the lush foliage that grows in the backyard, or she props herself against the tree reading and rereading her favorite book. On some nights her father goes into the garage more often than usual.

Several years later, the girl decides she is old enough to start her mornings by drinking coffee. She goes to the cupboard, pulls out a mug and pours herself a cup from the nearly full pot. Her father who is cooking their eggs says nothing, while her mother, who is never very talkative at that time of day, is engrossed in listening to the radio news. Soon her morning coffee becomes a habit, and day after day she sleepily pours herself a sloshed cup and wanders down the driveway to get the paper. During the spring and summer months when the mornings are pleasant, she doesn't bother to go back into the house, instead reads the comics and sips her coffee on the small patio where she feels more comfortable. The family dog, happy that someone is outdoors so early, always pesters her to play with him. She squats and rubs the dog's ears while speaking words of endearment, and on several occasions she is startled by her father coming out of the house, either on his way to get the car out of the garage, or to dump the garbage. She flushes when she realizes that as she sat on her heels, her father was able to see up her nightgown and she is wearing nothing underneath.

On the morning of her thirteenth birthday the girl receives a record player, and after this, she begins to stay indoors, spending her afternoons listening to music. As it is hot, she often removes her clothing and lies on her bed in her underwear and the bra she has just recently begun to wear. Sometimes she has to get up to use the bathroom and since her father is at work and her mother is in another part of the house, she doesn't bother to get dressed. Several times she has nearly collided with her father home early from work and walking down the carpeted hallway, where they both cried *oh*, and looked down at their feet.

When her brother returns home from college her father in-

73

dulges in beer openly, going down to the store before her brother is to arrive and returning home with several six-packs. Her mother does not seem to mind his drinking on these occasions and will occasionally join him, sipping a vodka collins. Her father and brother relax on the couch, quaffing from the brown bottles until her mother tells them both to use a glass. They eventually turn on the television news, leaning forward attentively during the segments about Vietnam, and talk mostly about her brother's grades, which if any lower could cause him to be drafted. When the conversation takes this direction her mother's face grows tense, she goes into the kitchen, returns with the vodka, collins mix and makes herself another drink. If the girl wanders into the room all three of them turn on her like she is an interloper and tell her to get out, that their discussion is none of her business. From different rooms in the house she can hear her brother indifferently rattling off his plan to go to Canada at the first communication from the draft board.

The following year the girl's parents call her down from her room to tell her that her father is moving out for a time, that they are going to have a trial separation. The girl sits there, unflinching, as her parents stare at her, expecting her to do or say something. She goes back to her room, puts on a record and throws herself on her bed. Over the last several months many of her classmates' parents have embarked on trial separations.

After her parents divorce, her father moves away and the girl rarely sees him, but when she does they are both uncomfortable. She asks him about his new job and life, while he asks her about school, making suggestions that she should try out for cheerleading, or band.

Her mother begins working in a housewares shop downtown, and the girl notices that after her mother has a job she is less critical of everything.

The girl's brother frequently stops off at the house for a few days during one of his hitchhiking trips. While their mother is at work they smoke a joint in the garden, then go in and listen to her Rolling Stones albums on the living room stereo.

When her brother is on the road again, the girl frequently goes cruising after school with an older boy, one of her acquaintances from the senior class. They drive around the main streets for a while, then take one of the roads leading out of town and park on a camouflaged access road. They drink beer and sometimes smoke pot if her friend has any, and then climb into the backseat of the car, where the girl removes her jeans and panties and vigorously slides up and down on the boy's penis, her arms thrown tightly, desperately around his neck, while the boy, eyes closed, intermittently shouts, *do it to me babe* over the music on the radio.

The Gift Horse's Mouth

HER FRIEND, A man who was once her lover, has given her a present for her birthday. They met for lunch, and he has walked her back to her apartment. He kisses her on the cheek, repeats *Happy Birthday*, hurries to the street corner to hail a cab.

Now in her living room, she takes a pair of scissors, cuts away the string and pulls the gift from its wrapping paper. The present is a beautiful lithograph, an abstract done in bright, primary colors. She is not surprised by this type of gift as her friend owns an art gallery. She looks at the signature, recognizes the artist's name. Her friend is dubious of this painter's work, has said that the work has real limitations. She wonders why he has made a gift of it. The artist may have sent the print to her friend as an offering, with the hope of someday showing in his gallery. She knows when he reviews work for exhibits, concludes that the lithograph had been sitting around in the back of the gallery collecting dust for half a year or more.

She is puzzled by his behavior: could giving her a gift he's contemptuous of be a sign of his hostility? He was friendly at lunch. Perhaps it is something else entirely—lack of money.

She picks up the print from the coffee table and puts it down again, now thinks it quite ugly. She gathers up the wrappings to toss into the dustbin when one of the pieces of paper catches her eye. It's a large sheet of cheap drawing paper—the kind used by art students for practice sketches. Her friend's handwriting fills one of the sides and she sits down to read what he has written. It seems to be the plot for a story about a man who wants to kill a woman he was once in love with because she knows all of his secrets, and could cause harm to his reputation.

When she had been intimate with her friend he'd showed no interest in writing, therefore he could have taken down an idea one of his colleagues had for a story, or it could be an idea for a performance piece. Or it's possible his wife decided that she would like to try her hand at writing and she'd dictated one of her ideas. But why sketch paper? He'd never kept that sort of paper around the gallery when the two of them were involved. . . She realizes there is a great deal she doesn't know about him in his present life, and that much time has passed since they'd been in love. All of the changes must have occurred during the year they didn't speak to one another. It's possible he might still bear some resentment toward her for not agreeing to his plan: he would marry his present wife, but the two of them would still continue their love affair. He was honestly surprised when his proposal made her incensed, was more surprised still when she threw cutlery at him, and was completely baffled when, several months later he called her up saying *Look, I've made a mistake. I never should have married____, can't we* and she'd slammed the phone down in disgust.

While staring at the lithograph, she remembers that her friend did once confess he'd wanted to strike her during one of their heated arguments, but he'd never done anything of the kind, and she'd never felt in any sort of danger around him. The secrets he'd confessed weren't anything more than what one person shares with another when they are close. He'd always been frightened of revealing himself though, and it was conceivable that he harbored animosity toward her for having done so.

She concludes his story, or whatever it is, is just some sort of fantasy, some sort of rebellious act done because his life has not turned out as happily as he'd expected.

She wants to forget about what he's written but the thought keeps nagging her: why had he wrapped the lithograph in it? An honest mistake? A welling up of subconscious behavior? Probably that.

She picks up the telephone, dials the gallery and when she hears him answer thanks him profusely for the lovely lithograph. Both of their voices are high and strained. After she hangs up, she takes the newspaper, opens it to the classified section and checks the listings of apartments for rent. All of the listings are very expensive. She's acting crazy. Why should she move out of her apartment just because of what is written on a piece of drawing paper?

She looks at the clock and sees she must get ready to meet a potential client about some freelance work. The man is pushy, loud and tries to get her to do the work for less money. After turning down the job she does not feel in the mood to return home, goes instead to a movie, a comedy that has recently opened. The movie is not funny. When the film concludes she walks back to her apartment and as she reaches it, is suddenly frightened and confused—thinks she has just glimpsed her former lover in front of her building. She stands in the street for a minute or so, walks in the opposite direction.

She wanders the streets of her neighborhood wishing to have dinner at a restaurant, but she must cook at home since she did not take the freelance work.

o o o

She is stirring some prepackaged ingredients into an instant rice dish when the telephone rings. It is her former lover. She looks at the clock, sees it's rather late. He sounds excited, and after several moments of small talk, pauses, and says he's just calling to see if everything is all right. She hesitates longer than she'd planned to before telling him everything is perfectly fine. He inquires if she had been out earlier. When she answers yes there is a long silence during which she tries to figure out the sub-text to his question, and his ensuing silence. When he speaks again it is to invite her to another lunch. She's vague about possible times and days, but he persists. Her instant rice burns while she looks through her appointment book.

The following Wednesday she meets him at a cafe where they always used to lunch. They make forced and nervous small talk. He adjusts his face to register surprise when she asks whether or not he's been in her neighborhood during the past two weeks. She recalls this look was always indicative of lying; he'd never gotten the startled, surprised part down correctly.

When they were involved she always took bites from his food and now she asks for a sample of his steak sandwich. He makes a gesture, indicating she should help herself. Instead of cutting off a bit of his lunch, she picks up his steak knife, swiftly inflicts a small cut on the index finger of his right hand. They stare at the spot until a sliver of blood oozes from it. He jumps slightly, puts his finger to his mouth.

They say goodbye in front of the cafe and neither mention what transpired inside. He heads back down the street toward the gallery and she walks in the other direction, thinks of getting a dog, or a stun gun.

o o o

Shall we meet again for another lunch, he asks. This time he suggests a Chinese restaurant, looks quite pleased with himself when he views the blunt wooden chopsticks on the table. He decides to order a bottle of wine, selects the most expensive on the menu. This makes her apprehensive, and she resolves to drink only one glass. But she is tense, unsettled—chastises herself for having agreed to see him again. By the time her entree arrives she's already halfway through her third glass of chardonnay.

Why did you give me an ugly, discarded print by an artist you think is talentless? she finally blurts. He looks genuinely puzzled, says he's always liked Sherman's work and she knows that. But the print he gave her was done by Blackwell. He looks confused and she doesn't believe he is acting. He mumbles something about having made an error, and if she returns the print he'll replace it with one by Sherman. They finish their wine in angry silence after she tells him she'd thrown it away the very day he presented it to her.

Blackwell's print was meant for a woman doing graduate work in art history. This woman had interviewed her friend for a small, underground art journal, and had expressed an interest in Blackwell's work during one of their meetings. Now this woman owns a print by Sherman. Her friend is reluctant to tell her the name of this graduate student, but she persists. The wine has broken down his reserve.

She thinks about Marie Masefield as she walks home from the Chinese restaurant and partly because she's been drinking, partly because she doesn't want to go home to more work, she enters a phone booth and looks through the directory. There is a listing for an M. Masefield on a street near the university, and she decides to walk over there, to walk off the wine if nothing else.

M. Masefield's building is one of those elegant structures that fell into disrepair, and recent efforts have been made to restore its gentility. She is surprised a graduate student can afford the rent in a building like this, but then it may well be another Masefield who lives here. She follows a man into the building—he even stops and holds the door open for her. She looks on the mailboxes, discovers Masefield lives in 18B. There is no telling whether or not the apartment belongs to Marie Masefield as the name on the box says only Masefield. Before she has the presence of mind to stop herself, she takes the elevator to the eighteenth floor, finds 18B, and puts her ear to the door. She hears muted jazz, wonders if anyone is there, or if this Masefield person leaves music on to discourage burglars. She pounds on the door, shouts, *Marie* and dashes around the corner. 18B opens slightly, but the person behind the door does not remove the chain.

One of the advantages of being a woman is that you're rarely seen as a threat. Would an unknown man have been able to sit on a bench in an apartment hallway for over an hour without causing comment? Not likely. She, however, is passed by several tenants who look right through her.

The door to 18B finally opens and a woman in her mid-twenties emerges. The woman charges to the elevator. Now that 18B has gone, she gets up and waits for the elevator to come back to the eighteenth floor. Once on the street she sees 18B. Why not catch up to her, ask her if she's Marie Masefield and if she is, tell her that their mutual friend has made a mistake, and that she is in erroneous possession of a Sherman print. But she does not do this, instead follows the woman into a coffee shop, a place that looks to be a student hangout. The woman sits down and appears to be waiting for someone—looks frequently at her watch and around the room. After a minute or so 18B pulls a book from her bag and begins reading. A closer look at the book might indicate if this is Marie Masefield, and so she walks by 18B's table. The book is something about art aesthetics, so it is quite likely the reader is Marie Masefield.

Losing her nerve to confront Marie Masefield about the Sherman print, she returns home, finds it disturbing that there are three hang-ups on her message machine. Though she now doubts that the caller is her former lover. Why would he bother calling, or surreptitiously hang about her building when Marie Masefield is his friend. It is clear, even after brief observation, that Marie Masefield is the way she herself used to be—buoyant, enthusiastic, energetic—how she was when she and her friend

82

initially became lovers.

She wants to see Marie Masefield and her friend together, and on an evening she knows her friend's wife attends an exercise class, she approaches the gallery. It is dark and closed for the night. Without hesitation she walks down the street to a bar where she and her friend met while his wife was exercising. The bar is not very crowded, most of the after-work crowd have gone some time ago. She selects a booth, decides she must confront herself about why she is so interested in Marie Masefield, and Marie's relation ship with her friend. She considers whether or not she might still be in love with her friend, or if her life has become so bland that Marie Masefield creates a diversionary interest, or if she needs to cling to the memory of her relationship with her former lover because no other has come along. She hears a laugh, not a polite, obligatory sort of laugh—a happy one. Marie Masefield's. She's in a corner booth with her—their friend. Her friend is pontificating; Marie is looking rapturously into his eyes, absorbing all he says as if his words are the wisest, most important in the world. Can there be a more stunning mirror in which he could view himself?

o o o

She decides that the best thing to do is apologize to her friend for disposing of Blackwell's print. She says she behaved badly, that she should have asked about the peculiarity of receiving a print by Blackwell. . .He accepts her apology and they're both silent.

She wonders if he is waiting for her to apologize for slicing his finger with the steak knife as well, but she also knows his line of thinking: he'd believe that her slicing his finger is indicative that she still cares.

Her friend is in the process of hanging a show, and as it is lunchtime, the artist wants to go to lunch. Her friend politely invites her along with them, but she declines, in turn politely promises to attend the show's opening.

She shouldn't be doing this. They could all return from lunch at any moment and find her here. She'd slipped unnoticed into the storeroom before the receptionist went out. Among the stretcher bars and old, peeling canvasses she has found sketch books—many of them, all filled with the same story: a man has to kill a woman he loves because he has allowed her to get too close, know him too well, and therefore she could do him harm. The stories take place in different settings and some have slightly different plots—variations on a theme, but the theme continually recurs.

She knows her friend and his receptionist will each blame each other for not activating the burglar alarm, and so she turns it off, disappears out the back door.

Sometimes it is best not to pursue things to their final conclusion. She is determined to put her friend, his sketchbooks and Marie Masefield out of her mind, refocus on her ordinary but relatively stable life. It is not difficult to do as her friend is busy with the show, and most likely with Marie, and he doesn't call.

One Saturday afternoon she walks home from a revival film being shown at the university and thinks of Marie Masefield. She recalls Marie lives nearby and decides to walk over to her building, return home by another route. The door of Marie's building is open and she walks in without hesitation, takes the elevator to the eighteenth floor and goes to 18B. The door is open and so she enters. There are drop cloths strewn about, and paint buckets in the center of the room. A man comes into the room and it is all she can do to keep from screaming. The man looks annoyed, tells her this apartment is not yet for rent; the apartment being shown is on the third floor and applications are on the kitchen counter. He adds that if she wants to look around, the apartment will be shown by the middle of the month, but there's already a waiting list. . . The man says he'll be back in a few minutes and tells her to make sure the door is locked when she leaves. She wanders around the living room and kitchen. Any sign of Marie, or Marie's life here has already been cleared away. She goes into the bedroom, it is spacious and light with an adjacent small balcony through a sliding glass door. . .the rent cannot be cheap. The room has not yet been cleaned or painted, and debris is laying about. A portion of the carpet is covered with shards of broken glass, and intermingled with the glass are fragments of paper—the images on the paper torn beyond recognition.

She looks out the bedroom window, sees that there is quite a decent view and opens the sliding glass door onto the balcony. She seats herself on the railing, carefully wraps her legs through the iron bars. The wind is sharper, more cold at this height, but the landscape and colors are expansive, bright. She makes small, tentative movements to overcome her fear at being up so high. Eventually she grows used to the elevation, is comfortable, begins to rock back and forth. As she gathers momentum her rocking becomes more and more furious. And she notices the air feels pleasant and cool in the spaces between her hands and the railing as she grasps the wrought iron with an increasingly relaxed grip.

Stranger Than Fiction

A MAN SHOUTS *lick my balls*. And a woman complies. As she is doing this she observes the protruding pale hairs, the testicles' pinkish brown color, the slight wrinkling of the skin, reminding her of elephant skin.

The man and woman continue to engage in sexual activity, and when the woman turns the page she drops the book on her lap, glances around to see if she has made a noise, perhaps uttered an *oh*. But the other passengers are absorbed in what they are doing, working on laptop computers, reading the paper, or dozing—and are not looking at her.

After the couple finished making love, the author described the male character's face as he sat with his back against the headboard; it is a face the woman knows quite well, belonging to someone exceptionally good-looking, with blonde hair, green eyes, a square, solid jaw, a tall, slim body and an irresistible voice—a voice that used to command her to *lick my balls*.

She thinks back to an earlier story in the collection, set in an area consisting of village-like towns, lying just north of a large city, adjacent to a bay. The fog came in in the evenings, causing the mountain looming high above the vicinity to disappear. At the time she thought it was just a coincidence, that the locale could just as easily be somewhere on the east coast. But between the landscape and this male character, could it be a story based on fact? She and the man she used to know lived just north of a city in a village-like town, adjacent to a bay and mountain.

The woman puts her bookmark in the book and turns to the author's biography. The author is a woman who currently resides in Michigan.

The bus arrives at her stop and she jumps out, hurries to work.

On the way home that evening, the woman can't wait to resume the story and opens the book while the bus is stuck in gridlock.

Ever since his youth, the male character has had the ability to get women to do what he wants—and what he wants is a great deal of sex, for women to dote on him.

They are crawling north on the freeway, passing through the county where the woman used to live, the one possibly described in the story. She passes through it five days a week on her way to and from her job in the city, which makes it too familiar to evoke any nostalgia or sentimentality—although she sometimes wishes she could live there again. But its being such a charming area also makes it an expensive one. For the last several years the woman has lived further north, in a county with many fast-food restaurants, hordes of crying or unruly children rolling around on shop floors, and men in large trucks who drive close to the shoulder of the road and scream *yeehaah* while she is riding her bike.

When the bus arrives at the depot, the woman gets off and goes to her car. She drives to an Italian deli, buys some dinner to reheat, heads to her small apartment, microwaves the manicotti and begins reading.

The story spans many years, with the man continuing to seduce large numbers of women, and shouting commands to them about what to do with his testicles—as well as other phrases like, *now, doggie style.* He keeps treating the people he is involved with badly—until he grows old and none will tolerate or take him seriously. But he still attempts to wield power over women, who if they pay him any heed at all, see him as a throwback from another era—or as mentally deranged. The story ends with several teenage girls wrinkling their noses in disgust and jaywalking when they catch the man, now elderly, leering at them while waiting for the pedestrian light to change.

The woman puts the book on her lap and thinks of some snapshots, undoubtedly lost—of her and the man with blonde hair posing knee-deep in the Pacific ocean, and holding beers at a party, the sun blazing behind them as they smiled into the camera. She is momentarily chagrined when she recalls how young they were, and how sophisticated and wise they believed themselves to be.

She has heard several reports from people she has run into, people she knew socially many years ago—that the man is successful, prosperous, and travels a great deal—to places like Berlin and Stockholm.

Like her, he has never married.

After the woman stopped seeing the exceptionally good-looking man, she lost interest in sex for a time, cut her hair and took up softball. When she occasionally spotted him—on the street or in a public place, she felt a rush of emotions, which led to quea-siness, and ducked down a side street, or left the building. Even-tually he moved away, and a year or so later she did as well, after which she didn't think of him very often.

Sometimes when she is in the area where she used to live, she finds herself keeping an eye out, wondering if his parents are still alive, and he might be in the area visiting them—and if the two of them would recognize one another.

The woman doesn't mind sitting on the bus during the long commute, for it gives her time to think, and after reading the story, she has been thinking about the way she was with the green-eyed man, the whirl of lust and abandon she felt when she was near him—how everything about him heightened her desire—the particular kind of soap he used, the smell of his hair, his taut belly. With every ensuing relationship, she felt less and less fer-vor—until the present where she can't muster the energy or en-thusiasm to go out on a date. It was not that she didn't feel sexual pleasure in the relationships that followed, but it wasn't the same. With each new entanglement she sensed that her psyche had be-come a bit harder. She still liked sex, at least the last time she had it she remembered liking it, but in the same way she enjoyed exercise, and the sensation following any sort of workout—the sense of invigoration and elevation in mood.

If not for that, she doubts she would ever sleep with men again.

When she played softball, she rememberd the hostility and contempt the men on her team, and the opposing one, showed if women players did too well—hit runs off their pitches, or caught their in or out-of-bounds hits. If the male members of the team made these plays, that was one thing, but if it was a woman, she noted the rage on a man's red face, witnessed an out-of-control male firing a ball, throwing a bat, or trying to hit a woman with a softball if he was pitching and she was poised at the plate. *This is real*, she recalls thinking all those years ago. *This has nothing to do with who wins at softball.*

The woman is riding her bike late one afternoon. When she is stopped at a red light at a busy intersection with a line of cars behind her, she sees a silver Jaguar travelling north through the intersection. A man is behind the wheel, a good-looking man with blonde hair and sunglasses, his left arm out the window. Several seconds later the car behind her blows his horn for her to go and she sees the light has turned green. For an instant she thinks it is the man she knew. As she pedals along the side of the road she tells herself that he probably no longer looks like that, could very likely now be bald and insecure, and what could the odds be that it really was him cruising through the intersection?

The stoplights and signs become fewer until she is riding in the country, pumping smoothly and rhythmically. This is one of the favorite aspects of my life, she thinks. As she rides, she allows herself to admit that she made the man up; she did it a long time ago and held the illusion for all these years. He was someone she once found physically attractive, but the other attributes she'd given him were things she'd fabricated in order to designate her first rush of desire.

At the top of a steep hill she stops, catches her breath and drinks some water from a plastic bottle attached to her bike. As she begins the descent, she begins to feel exhilarated from the speed she is accumulating. It is what makes climbing worthwhile.

While racing down the hill she dodges rocks on the road and flashes on the command the character in the story uttered, what a man in real life said also. Why did the author have the fictional female think of elephants? What could she know of them?

The woman knows nothing of them, but is somewhat familiar with the story of an elephant-headed Hindu god with the body of a man who holds in his belly all the orbs of destruction, to be set upon the world if his wrath is incurred. Yet he is considered one of the more affable deities.

When the road levels off, the woman begins again to pedal, a steady pace that takes her further and further into the countryside, with its crisp blues and greens—apparently bucolic and seemingly benign.

Budget Cuts

THE ECONOMY WORSENED so the government threatened to cut social programs, to discontinue educational loans and student grants, to remove underprivileged children from their parents and build large, costly orphanages to sequester them, and to cut all funding for art and culture. Then they voted themselves large pay-raises.

People grew angry and afraid. Those who participated in self-destructive or anti-social behavior shot more people.

Those who were artists became more overtly hostile and frantic. If one artist had more showings than another, or received better reviews, the former artist would become exceedingly friendly with the latter and invite her to his studio. When the latter artist accepted, and arrived bringing cheese or scones or some other little gift for the occasion, the former artist would ask the more successful to be seated, pour the refreshment, then go into a long, resolute diatribe about how it was certainly apparent that the more successful artist was color-blind and practically incapable of holding a paintbrush.

Some textual artists wrote self-pitying tomes that pointed out the obvious. When these tomes failed to attract any interest whatsoever, the artists became furious, disbelieving, and put it down to being misunderstood—so self-absorbed that they failed to realize the cliché of that thought. Others, those who once dabbled at being artists and afterward took jobs as receptionists in galleries, kept a vigilant eye out to make sure that no former art-school classmate establishing a career would slip a portfolio or slides through to the owner and ever get a show in *that* gallery.

Certain writers tended to use slightly more subtle, less guerrilla-like tactics. When no one was looking they scuttled into book shops and slipped their books onto Staff Recommendation shelves, or wrote essays that began as homages to famous writers and concluded as glowing reviews of their own work. Many who wrote only now and again, and lacked belief in what they did, shoved their work into drawers and devoted their time to compiling lists of typos in published books—and faxed their findings to various publishing houses at the end of each working day.

Young artists who felt they weren't getting anywhere in their careers abandoned trying to display their creations altogether and took to the streets wearing sandwich boards that read, PAY ATTENTION TO ME. Pedestrians in certain neighborhoods took them to be performance artists and threw change at them, ensuring that certain artists at least had enough pocket change to go for a coffee or a beer.

Most artists, though, borrowed a page from corporate America and read books like *How to Work a Room, Dress for Success* and *Don't Make Waves, Make Money.* Some went to therapists or counselors who told them, "Imagine it, Feel it, Be it"— and afterward strutted around as if they were famous and triumphant—and fooled some of the people some of the time. Most though, merely smiled and said sweet but insincere things to almost everyone with any sort of power, even the most infinitesimal shred of influence, hoping with increasing desperation for just one tiny, tiny piece of the pie.

Somebody somewhere thought that Somebodies somewhere, probably southern republican politicians, were slapping High Fives at that very minute.

Bond

YOUR HUSBAND HAS become a dour person who starts arguments, always believes he's right and comes up with strange, incomprehensible reasons for doing what he does.

You remember when the sound of his voice aroused you, how the touch of his hand on your arm made your pelvis go soft—and now, when looking across the room at him, his presence fills you with revulsion and chagrin.

Sometimes you have the urge to go up to him and shout: *why do you wear the same dirty clothes,* or *why don't you bathe more often!*

On evenings when the sight of him is more irritating than usual, you jump up and say *I'm going out.* But once out, there is the problem of not having a place to go, the town is small and closes down at 9:00 p.m.—with the exception of several bars with bad reputations.

You move down the street, pass people walking their dogs, you and the animal owners nod to each other. You return home, go to bed early.

In late winter, after the rains, you walk down a street in the heart of town and discover a place with neon bulbs in front and lights on inside. It is a newly-opened cafe. You look around, hoping you are not the oldest one here, for there are many young, sullen-looking people sitting about.

A man sits down at a table several feet from yours, glances around to see if anyone is looking at him and meets your eyes. He is instantly distracted by several people who come and join him. When you finish your tea, you slowly walk back home, savoring the time, and for some reason are not apprehensive about walking the dark, deserted streets alone. As you open the door you feel sorry—and guilty for the thoughts you have about your husband.

You begin to go to the cafe several nights a week. One evening, your husband gets up and follows you, trailing about fifty yards behind. You fantasize about leading him on a wild goose chase, you and he going around and around until midnight, when you would both be cold, and his back would ache, as it always does when he walks more than a block. You arrive at the cafe, order your tea and sit down. As your husband passes he stops, cranes his neck and stares in the French window. The silver teapot feels good in your hands, hot and comforting. Your eyes meet his as you bring the cup of tea to your lips. Both of you pretend not to know one another and he turns away, continues down the street. When you arrive home neither of you mention what transpired.

After several months of sitting in the cafe alone, the young man comes up and seats himself at your table. At first you are nervous, think of jumping up and leaving. But the man says. *Hello I'm* _____. You guess him to be in his early twenties, and notice his scent—soap, and fresh ironing, a smell quite different from your husband's. You are happy he is here. He says he noticed you have been coming into the cafe, and he would like to know about you. *There is not much to tell.* You are married, have a job that is not particularly interesting or lucrative. You trail off, shrug your shoulders, look at him to see if you can deduce what he wants to find out, but he begins telling you about himself: he has ambitions which lie in the direction of painting and acting, and he can't decide which to pursue. You are surprised he has read as many books as he has, has read them seriously, some of which are difficult; many he read in his mid-teens.

Outside the cafe, you wonder about what the young man might want from you, aside from being able to impress his circle that he can go up to a woman who is older than he is, sit down and she does not ask him to leave.

When you return home, your husband is sitting on the couch, looking very tired.

Sometimes when the young man talks, you have the impulse to touch him, have difficulty deciding whether you want to do this in a sexual or nonsexual way, for if you were to touch him in a sexual way, it could lead to sex, maybe once, maybe more than once; the sex might be good, involving many pleasant orgasms. You would get used to each other's bodies, grow comfortable. The allure would either wear off, or it wouldn't. What difference would it make?

You think about leaving your husband, of entering into a chaste relationship with the young man, where you would watch him, smell his smell of laundered clothing, freshly washed skin and listen to him talk from his state of promise.

While sitting in the living room, you read a story by Ingeborg Bachmann about a man whose wife bears him a son. When the little boy is still a toddler the man loses interest in him, can already tell that there is nothing different about the boy. At the end of the story the boy dies by slipping during a field trip and hitting his head on a rock. You carry the story in your mind for days, and one evening in the cafe, repeat it to the young man. He does not understand why you are telling it, and you are not sure either, except that you do not think he is destined to live reflexively. *Escape. Get away,* you want to shout, but he will think you mean he should leave the small town, try to make his way in a big city.

The television is on and you sit beside your husband watching the evening news. You raise your arm as if to put it around his shoulders, instead put your hand on the back of his neck and pull so the loose, crêpey skin on the front of his neck becomes taut and his Adam's apple juts out. He goes into the bedroom and slams the door behind him.

In late spring you resolve not to return to the cafe, for you do not want to run into the young man in three years, or perhaps five, walking about town in the attire of a salesperson, ashamed of your encountering him on a tree-lined street, with a pleasant looking wife in tow and a baby who fusses and drools. Now you are free to imagine that the young man will get the life he wants, will not be beaten down by disappointment, will stay unscathed, unthwarted, and poised on the threshold.

Summer is hotter than any on record, making it difficult to sleep. Night after night you lie beside your husband, who tosses and sweats, or you don't go to bed at all, lie on the couch listening to night sounds until the early morning when car doors begin opening, motors rev up and commuters race toward the highway in the semidarkness.

On an evening when no breeze blows through the small house, despite opening all the windows and both the front and back doors, your husband decides to rent a film. He inserts a video tape into the VCR, a movie he has always wanted to see called *Jonah Who Will be Twenty-Five in the Year Two Thousand*, about a group of sixties activists and what became of them following those years of unrest. He does not like the strange cuts, and thinks the story line too rambling so the point is diluted. When it is over he sits back and sighs, for he had been part of the sixties. He gets off the couch and rewinds the tape. After he puts the tape back in its box, you take your husband's hand, something you have not done in a long time, and lead him to the bedroom. While he plays with your breasts and suckles your nipples you do some mental calculations, deduce that the young man from the cafe will be twenty-seven in the year 2000, and as you and your husband have sex, you contemplate how much of your life will have gone by when the millennium arrives.

A Fiction

PERHAPS THE MAN was right, the stories were not good. She had shown the man other stories, which he said he enjoyed, but perhaps he hadn't really liked those either. Perhaps he had only pretended to like the stories so she would continue to have sex with him. It's possible that when she stopped sleeping with the man, he no longer found her stories of interest. True, she did not believe the stories finished, but could they be as appallingly bad as he implied? She'd showed this group of stories to several men and women who said they liked them—and they hadn't indicated any sexual interest in her.

The woman decided to put aside her writing for that day, to go for a walk, clear her head, and maybe get a perspective on what she'd written.

As she strode around the town, she passed a candy store and was tempted to buy a dozen or so Molasses Chips. But while looking inside the shop window, she acknowledged that eating candy would not make the man like the stories any better, nor help her gain confidence in them.

As she crossed to the next block, she passed a café with outdoor seating and saw several young men of the town gathered about a table. They called her over to their group to tell her they had formed a band, and that they had seen several of her stories published in a magazine. They said they liked them. Continuing on her walk, she thought that the young men were probably sincere; she couldn't believe they would want her for a sex partner—for there were young women in their circle, all quite attractive and nubile.

The woman entered the park where joggers, tennis players, people on skates and walkers congregated after work. She fell in behind some race-walkers and tried to keep up. While pushing with her calves and pumping her arms, she remembered another man she used to have sex with, long ago. He made derisive comments when she arrived back at their apartment, sweaty and exhilarated from jogging. One time, however, he asked to go along. She was rather startled when he met her in the park after work wearing street clothes and combat boots, informing her that this was his running attire. He shouted marching Military Cadence songs as they made their way over the paths, and toward the end of the workout, with about an eighth of a mile remaining, he began to sprint—his boots made divots in the cinder path, the tail of his sweat-soaked dress shirt flapped out behind him, the military slogans were unrecognizable through his gasps. When they returned to her car he gloated over winning. His bragging startled her for she'd made a special effort to run more slowly than usual—the man was unexercised, twenty years her senior and she had feared he might drop dead.

While passing by the tennis courts she saw a group lesson in progress, the instructor putting the students through a series of drills. Watching this activity triggered her memory of another man, a man with a German accent. She had met him while playing tennis, and dated him several times, until he had asked her one evening, over dinner, why she wasted money on tennis lessons, that it was obvious she'd reached her potential and wouldn't get any better. After she stopped seeing the man, she found out from other tennis enthusiasts that the man was a womanizer, with a penchant for Catholic schoolgirl outfits and whips.

While the woman maintained her quick pace out of the park en route to her apartment, she tried to determine why her participation in various activities had annoyed so many. She hadn't made it known to anyone when some of her pieces appeared in literary journals, how many miles she'd logged in that week, or given progress reports on her overhead smash.

At a red light she had the recollection of another man she'd known when she was twenty, a professor at her art college who took up drinking after an acrimonious divorce; he often invited her and several others to drop by his studio to drink beer. A week after she'd received first place in the annual student exhibition, he'd arrived at the afternoon painting class semi-intoxicated, and ridiculed her canvases. She never returned to the school, gave up painting for a year and finally graduated from another institution.

Upon reaching her apartment building, the woman bounded up the stairs to the third floor, and while walking down the hallway thought perhaps it was the involvement, not the activity, that had angered so many—that while she was absorbed in it she did not think of anyone or anything else. If that were true, though, men (who'd married wives who'd given up their own interests in the name of commitment) would not have rung her bell during the evening hours, waving champagne bottles, saying their wives used bad grammar, habitually watched television and were boring—and did she have any interest in a little champagne, followed by sex?

The woman went to the sink and washed her face. She opened the refrigerator, poured herself a glass of mineral water from the chilled bottle and went back to her desk. She read, again, the stories in question.

She thought it probable the man resented how she'd changed; when they'd first met she lacked self-assertion and direction in her life, was often given to nervous laughter, and rarely verbalized what she really thought. He liked her better in those days.

The woman read the stories over several more times and now believed them finished. She speculated that someday she might read this group of fictions at a reading, or send them out to several editors to get their reaction. The sun, low in the sky, radiated through the kitchen window filling the room with early-evening light. She sipped her water and envisioned someone someday liking the stories enough to publish them in a collection, where they would exist as accounts of a fictive past. But a printed and bound collection would be very much in the present, a present where she could exist only as a body of work. . .merely as words, lines and apperceptions making their way into the world.

Sometimes on Saturday

MID-MORNING WE are watering the garden. The fog has just lifted and it looks to be a nice day. The roses are doing well, the rosemary is blooming, as is the dianthus. There is a noise, probably a car in the driveway, someone lost. A car door slams, and then another. Girl Scouts? Campfire Girls selling candy? No, not Girl Scouts, adults, four of them. Four adults holding pamphlets. We can tell from their dress and their demeanor that they want to spread the word of God. They knock on the front door. We are silent, still peeking from behind a corner of the house. The front door is locked, and as no one is inside to answer it, they will soon go away. But they do not go away. They survey the property. Here they come, how did they spot us? We dodge behind the house again, hearing footsteps. They outnumber us—what to do? One of us pulls open a door that leads underneath the house and crouches in the basement, trying to breathe as quietly as possible. It is cool here. Through the thin crack where the door is warped one of us sees one of them: gray trousers, pamphlet still in hand searching behind the rose bushes.

While one of us dives into the basement, the other makes for the tall grass behind the garage, and lies there trying to decide what to say if discovered: *We don't want any?* The dry grass crackles with footsteps none too far away.

Eventually we hear the car doors slam again, and the sound of a vehicle exiting the driveway. Cautiously, we come out of our hiding places, dust ourselves off and rendezvous. We go to the front porch and remove the pamphlet they have left. There is no point in talking to them, for they do not take no for an answer.

We return to the garden, victorious on yet another Saturday morning.

Cow

THROUGH THE WINDOW I see a black Angus cow lying sick in the pasture across the road. A large group of Angus stand near it, watching. The farmer comes out of his house and looks at it also. He stands in front of the cow for several minutes, kneels at its side. The rest of the herd moves closer. The farmer prods the cow and its legs strike out. I hope he is not causing her to suffer. Apparently the farmer does not know what is wrong and continues poking at her. She doesn't move and I think he has killed her, as a sick cow would be of no use to him. But eventually the animal moves its head and I am quite relieved. The herd has formed a tight circle around the farmer and the cow. When the farmer becomes aware of this, he gets up, runs in circles waving his arms and shoos them away.

The telephone rings and I speak to a business associate, a former love. His dourness is irritating, and throughout our conversation I think of ways to find a new business associate to perform that particular job for the organization.

The farmer goes to the barn, returns holding a rope and circles the cow. He tries to get the animal on its feet by putting the rope around her body and pulling, but the cow only flails a little; the farmer looks quite exerted and frequently wipes his brow. Soon after, the farmer goes back to the barn and comes out driving a tractor. He drives the tractor toward the cow and I wonder if he is going to try and scoop her up and drive off, but he sits in the tractor for a long time doing nothing while the tractor runs and the cow stays prone.

He finally hops off the machine, and kneels next to the beast, blocking my view. I cannot tell what the farmer is doing, if he is giving her a euthanizing injection, or if he is trying to revive her.

The telephone rings again and the caller is someone I used to love and might still love. Throughout the conversation I watch the man and cow, but do not mention either to the person I am speaking to.

After hanging up, I work at the computer, looking up occasionally to check the progress of the man and cow. The man climbs back onto the tractor and returns to the barn. The rest of the herd has wandered off and I take this as an indication the animal is dead, or dying. The farmer comes out of the enclosure, leans on a fence and stares at the creature for a long time. He goes away and I don't see him again.

Minutes later a large vulture alights on a fence near the animal. My stomach feels queasy, but I've been drinking coffee all morning.

Several more vultures glide by the creature and I feel badly for her—her misery. Just when I've given up on the cow, I see her raise her head for a minute or so, only to collapse again a few minutes later.

I'm depressed, but have been since Monday.

I'm tempted to call back the person I used to love and might still love, as he could comfort me. But our relationship doesn't work that way and he would undoubtedly be annoyed, as he is also working and we spoke a mere half an hour ago.

I finish the work I've been doing, highlight "save" and turn off the computer. I see from the hour that I must get ready to go to a meeting.

I wonder if at the meeting I will find someone to love, someone who would also love me, or if not that, if I will meet someone who will listen with either real or polite interest when I relate there is a black Angus cow lying dead in the field across the road from where I'm living.

Hangman

THEY HAVE BEEN best friends since they were nine, and during every study hall have surreptitiously played the game of Hangman. They are so quiet and practiced they have never been caught. At the end of the seventh grade one of the girls is distracted and bored with the game, but plays anyway, sloppily marking the binder paper with lines where the letters will go, while looking around the study hall in the hope that a particular boy is watching her. She smiles at the boy and crosses her legs so her skirt rises to reveal her thighs. Each time her friend guesses a letter, the figure of the hanged man receives another embellishment. Finally the stick figure is complete and the girl writes: *You lose,* displaying the word her friend was supposed to deduce. *But you misspelled it!* her friend shouts, causing the teacher to rush over and make black marks next to their names in her book.

One of the girls spends the summer on the other coast, and that fall they encounter each other on the first day of school. Over the summer the girl who drew the hangman developed breasts, while her friend got acne. The former girl walks past her friend and joins a group of eighth grade females who also have breasts, who are also wearing dresses and makeup. They form a tight cluster next to the lockers, talk and laugh among themselves. Instinctively the other girl goes toward some students she has known since the fourth grade, girls who are either pre-pubescent, wear braces, glasses, or have imperfect skin.

Although they know they are too old for it these girls go to the playground, swing from the monkey bars, or rock up and down on seesaws. Bored with this, they drag their shoes through the coarse sand. As dust flies they become increasingly frenetic, begin running haphazardly around the playground, their arms outstretched. *Ugly bitch* they shout and scream while trying to knock one another down in the dirt.

An Adolescence

THE GIRL SITS on the couch reading a novel, enjoys the spooky Gothic setting, and pretends there is a madwoman locked in her attic. But the house she lives in does not have an attic, so she imagines the crawl space between the roof and the ceiling as adequate to hide someone's dark secret. As she turns the pages she munches on junk food, washing it down with soda water, taking comfort in the fact that although she is not beautiful, she might someday have an interesting life and walk on uninhabited moors. In the backyard her father is mixing cement to lay a path, while her mother plants tulips. Her parents forever work at home improvement.

o

The girl and her mother sit in the pediatrician's office while the doctor is provoked into loudly and emphatically lecturing on the benefits of physical activity, and the evils of junk food, pronouncing that the girl must immediately begin a regimen of exercise.

o

In a dimly lit, cavernous rink, the girl skims over the ice, her ankles turning inward, her arms flailing for balance. When the session is over she hands in her skates at the rental booth in the lobby while her mother, who has come to drive her home, questions her suspiciously: how many times did you go around? Her parents do not want to pay money for her to circle the rink over and over again, only to find out that she had gone into the heated women's restroom and sat on the bench reading Gothic romances. When they arrive home, her mother drifts outside to help her father add a new coat of white paint to the fence, and the girl settles onto the couch.

o

She is careful to order only fruit salad and a glass of skim milk, so her skating coach will not think that she eats too much, that she is serious about her training. Her mother and coach talk of people from the rink and various other subjects. In the booth next to the girl are her custom-made skates, which she didn't want to leave in the car, the blades press cold against her thighs.

o

They are celebrating that several hours previously the girl became a sliver medallist in the Central Pacific junior ladies competition, but instead of cake, the girl orders a salad with low-fat dressing—to show her coach and mother that she is not willing to rest on her laurels. She mustn't squander her chances, her coach reiterates, especially since she has blossomed physically.

o

A sad case, her coach explains, referring to their waitress. Her husband left her for another woman and ran off with all their money. That is why she is forced to wait tables. She has given up, her coach whispers, that is why she grows fatter and fatter. Very sad, yes, the girl and her mother agree, keeping their voices low, careful not to look in the woman's direction. The girl drinks black coffee and nibbles at a few crackers, thinking she will never give up, no matter what.

o

Not a Yorkshire moor, but the girl stands on a sidewalk, in hip-hugger slacks, and platform shoes, hitchhiking under a spring sun. She knows she will have no trouble getting a ride—not from the type a nineteenth century novelist might have devised, but from one suntanned man or another who will stop his Porsche, Corvette, or M.G. convertible, ask her destination, light a joint, take a few hits and pass it to her, saying she shouldn't hitchhike, and it's really lucky a nice guy like himself picked her up.

Said driver in his predictable sports car is disappointed to learn that she is underage, drops her at her destination and roars off.

o

Her parents make enough home improvements to sell the house for a nice profit, and buy a bigger house in a more exclusive neighborhood. They no longer plant trees or paint fences, instead hire gardeners and workmen for such projects, while they ride their bicycles, sun by the pool or prepare to go out for dinner. The young woman's room is a converted attic, with a skylight and large bay windows. The young woman and her friend hang out one of these windows, exhaling an exotic substance so no one can detect the smell. When they are finished the young woman tips the small, gold pipe so the ashes go floating down near the little sports car her parents bought her—which she will drive to the beach as soon as the Patti Smith album comes to an end.

o

He is as handsome and brooding as any literary hero—and prone to fits of rage, which he is now exhibiting as he knocks her to the asphalt path in the park where she skins her back and begins to scream. The cause of his torment is her refusal to have sex with him in the back of his car, for she thinks they will be detected by the police who patrol the area. But he is drunk, horny, and the thought of possible detection is titillating.

o

At 2:00 a.m. in a twenty-four hour coffee shop, the handsome young man who is prone to brooding and fits of rage—and his best friend—order bacon, eggs, hash browns and coffee. Out of habit the young woman only has tea and a glass of water. She wonders if the waitress recognizes her as the girl who used to go into that other coffee shop in her skating outfit. But if so, the waitress doesn't let on.; instead she turns her face into a mask as the best friend of the bad tempered man mercilessly derides her about her enormous girth—then repeatedly shouts what a great idea it would be for her to perform a blow job on him when she finishes work. The young woman would like to shout, *shut up, just shut up,* but does not have the courage. She knows that if she just keeps dieting, is polite and self-effacing, that she will probably be exempt from enduring what the waitress is having to endure.

o

Her parents sell the new house for an even larger profit and move to a much smaller place in the country. Once there, they resume hauling rocks, planting flowers, and adding decks. That fall, the young woman goes off to college. She no longer wears platform shoes and tight hip-hugger slacks. Instead, she prefers jeans, tennis shoes and a man's gray overcoat she found at a used clothing store. On the first day of her English class, she is given a syllabus, finds she is required to write a paper on "Feminist Paradigms, The Body of the Text, and The Unconscious in Nineteenth Century Gothic Romance."

o

Nothing seems real anymore. She turns in her assignments, receives good grades, hurries to get away from campus and walks around in a fog. The world, she thinks, looks like a gelatin silver print.

What her peers think is fun, she has already experienced—the parties, the wildness. Of her professors, she marvels that so many can be paid for such mediocrity, and she sits through class after class, after a time only halfway conscious of the droning.

o

A man somewhat older, for they are always older, asks her to dance in a cafe with ferns. There is jazz playing. She wonders why men think they have the right to come up to women they do not know, as if a woman's sole reason for venturing into public places is to have men disturb their thoughts. She wants to ask: why isn't the man's overcoat strewn over my chair, my not wearing makeup, a sign to you that I no longer want to be part of the game?

The man offers her drugs, thinking perhaps this will be sufficient motivation for her to dance with him. She leaves the cafe, ducking down a side street to make sure she is not followed.

o

Next to the river there is a bookstore with an adjacent cafe. She and her friend meet there, show one another books they've purchased that have nothing to do with their curriculum, making these titles more interesting. Sometimes men come up to them (odd since they both dress in army fatigues and ripped T-shirts) and want to partake in their conversation. She tells a man and her friend about Max Ernst's *Un Semaine de Bonté*, how it is composed in different sections, and Ernst substituted the seven deadly sins for seven deadly elements—water, fire, etc. The collages are comprised of nineteenth century pulp fiction. . . terror, torrid love, torture. The man says she does not have to talk about such lofty things as art. *But I like art!* she exclaims. Soon the man grows hostile; she and her friend are hurrying out the door and running to their car as he follows them.

○

In summer her parents vacation in the mountains and invite her along. She in turn asks her friend to accompany her. She and her friend sit by the lake and smell the pine scent floating from the trees. Sometimes they go to a rustic bar to play pool in the late afternoon. The people here assume she and her friend are lesbians. The resort community is very small, provincial.

On one occasion they stay at the tavern and play pool later than usual, until disco music blares from the jukebox. Once outside, they discover they have been followed, again find themselves breaking into a run, this time with a good head start, and dive into some shrubbery. The woman is quite pleased her friend has begun to study kung fu, but utilizing her new skills does not prove necessary, as the man staggers past the foliage and into the night.

o

The woman wonders why, since there are many women in the United States who wear makeup, high heels, tight jeans and have cute haircuts, she and her friends find themselves leaving early, often apprehensively and frequently at a trot—places where they bother no one and do not seek attention. Perhaps it is because they break the female dress code. But certain women have been doing that for years. Perhaps it is because the word statutory no longer serves to protect them.

o

After a long interval she allows a man into her life again, a once-known actor in the local theatre, who has performed many dramatic and comedic roles—but has recently found himself cast in fewer and fewer parts. He takes to pretending he is a star and parades around her apartment in fright wigs and lederhosen, or the tights of a Shakespearean actor—which he finds sexually arousing and she finds unbecoming. He mumbles partially recalled soliloquies, but eventually forgets those as well. In his frustration he calls her names, makes fun of her accomplishments.

Noted: even a fool can wield a sword.

Surrounded by books, so many books, they make the walls vibrant with color, although the room is dark and drab. All grown-up and surrounded by books in a little room.

Kind of a life, she thinks, a kind of life. A good life.

Another one is not really imaginable, thinks the embodiment from her chair. Outside there are traffic sounds, sirens, occasional gunfire, but within the four walls their sounds seem staged, as if coming from props.

What would happen were she to venture out of the room? Would she evanesce, as she so often imagines?

More sounds of traffic and urban noise filters in amidst the brightly colored book spines on the shelves.

When young, she had no idea how dark it was inside the body.

70s Soul

THE COAST IS gray and foggy. We walk for awhile, looking out at the iron-gray water. As we move further down the beach we want to get some protection from the wind and walk near the dunes, averting our eyes when we come upon someone injecting himself behind a rock. We return to the car, chilled from the cold and damp.

On the other side of the hill the sun reemerges. We have begun to listen to a program on public radio, a segment of soul music from the seventies. The good old days, she says, the days when we could sleep with anyone and not fear dying. My friend and I hardly have time to see each other anymore. The weather is pretty, I've rolled back the sunroof, and we're hearing music from our youth. The songs remind me of the beach, a different beach, of times when my friend and I took our transistor radios to the coast, set the dial on the local FM station that played sets of Al Green, The Spinners, The Stylistics. We often took the radio with us while we walked, barefoot, on the hard-packed sand by the water's edge. It never occurred to us that one day beach shoes would be *de rigueur*. I remember the clothing we practically lived in at the time, cutoffs and halter tops, and the suntans we culti-vated. Sun exposure was considered pleasurable, healthy, the sun a good source of vitamin D.

I point out the obvious: of course those times seemed more carefree, they were—we were quite young. But my friend objects, says it was more than that—people were less hostile, they enjoyed their lives more. *The economy* we say in unison. We know that ours is the first generation in this country that will not exceed the wealth of its parents, that by the time we reach retirement age the Social Security reserves will be depleted through government borrowing. However, the day is so pretty, here, twelve miles from the coastline, that we drop the subject, grow quiet and continue to listen.

When Marvin Gaye's "Let's Get it On" plays, my friend, who is lounging with the passenger seat tilted back, asks quietly if I have a picture of the 70s as they really were, when women routinely had sex with men they didn't like and weren't attracted to. She talks about the subtle coercion, how sex was always expected on a date—or when sex *was* the date, accompanied by alcohol and drugs. She dredges up the memory of those parties where everyone jumped into the hot tub. My friend talks of how, if you didn't engage in casual sex, you were considered weird, neurotic. The words "hung-up" and "uptight" were leveled against you. My friend is angry. She has worked herself up. *Pull over,* she demands, as we're about to pass a mini-mart. She comes out with a pack of cigarettes, although she hasn't smoked in years. We try and resolve what to do when she wants to smoke in my car and I don't want her to. *I'm not pregnant yet,* she states defensively as she gets out of my car and leans on it, puffing away. She puts the cigarette out before it's finished as it's making her sick. Back on the road we listen to the final set of the program and cringe when recollecting a piece of vernacular from that time: "jump your bones." Did we have sex with anyone who used that expression? We hope not. We can't remember.

We are relieved when the next radio program comes on—it is Andrei Codrescu talking about vampires.

I pull up in front of my friend's building. She hasn't been feeling well, has been made anxious and upset by the procedures she's undergoing for in vitro fertilization. We walk up the steps to her apartment and I look at her the way I would someone I didn't know. When did we start dressing like this, wearing dark colors, loose-fitting clothing, black leather coats, sturdy boots, and dark glasses to avoid eye contact with strangers?

While my friend is rustling through her purse for her keys, I lean forward and kiss her on the back of the neck. She doesn't say anything and I think she is going to pretend I didn't do it, but when we're inside her apartment she locks the door, goes to the bathroom, turns on the shower and begins throwing off her heavy, black clothes. I trail after her and stand in the doorway, watching. She impatiently moves past me, motions me to get out of the way, secures the bathroom door and steps into the shower. I also remove my garments, feel the rush of hot water. We wash one another, removing the ocean's salty stickiness from our faces, hair and hands—wash one another and kiss. Surrounded by steam and coral-colored tile, we forget the father of her soon-to-be in vitroized child—her husband, and the layers of our bleak conversation.

Neck and Neck

HEAD STUCK THROUGH two metal bars, and it does not move. A woman passes at a good clip, turning the pedals of her bicycle. Day after day she races past the creature, her legs moving up-and-down like piano keys, while the animal remains still. She is fairly certain the sheep can withdraw its head and settle back into the confines of the enclosure.

The woman is away a long while, riding into town to do errands, on some days riding past the town entirely, for pleasure, a sense of doing something different and doubles-back to do the things she must do in the village. When she returns home many hours later the sheep is in the same position.

The animal has a trough of water and a semi-enclosed shelter within the pen, where its food must be kept, for it does not look emaciated.

On a couple of occasions the woman has gotten off her bicycle and stopped to watch the sheep while drinking water from a plastic bottle. It looked back without interest, or desire for attention, unlike other farm animals, horses and cattle, that often press against fences when she stops on the deserted country roads.

The sheep is not a particularly attractive animal, it has black markings on its ears, face and legs, which give it a rather mottled look—and flat eyes that are inscrutable, sheep-like, with their rectangular pupils.

In the town the woman does banking and shops for groceries, carrying her purchases in a large pack on her back. She also frequents the bicycle shop where she buys new tubes, and the management lets her work on the gears, replace the valves and rim strips on her tires.

Sometimes the woman rides into the town and does not do errands, or work on her bike. Instead, she goes into a cafe, has a cup of coffee and waits. When a man arrives they sit and talk for an hour or so before leaving. He fastens her bike to the back of his car and they go to his house, where she performs fellatio.

After this occurred several times she asked the man when he was going to do sexual things to her. He said, *soon, soon,* but he had to ease into it.

At other times the woman goes into the cafe and when the man comes in they drink coffee, afterwards play chess at a corner table. When she wins she scrutinizes him carefully, looking for a sign that he might be sulking or annoyed.

On the way to-and-from town, she has, on more than one occasion, wondered about the sex of the sheep, once nearly crashing while leaning over at a precarious angle, trying to discern the genitals.

The woman finds out from a farmer that the breed of sheep with black markings is a Dorset Down originating in England in 1834, a hybrid of the Leicester Longwool and a breed she has already forgotten.

She doesn't feel any fondness or real interest in the creature.

It has become no friendlier since she began stopping near it to drink her water, and she finds it faintly irritating that it is always sticking its head out of the pen, since there is nothing she can do. If she went into the enclosure and set it free, it could be hit by a car, or attacked by one of the dogs that live on the many farms in the area.

Maybe the creature is doleful and absurd in its sheepness. She will no longer look over when she rides, for she does not want to fly past it, bearing witness to its existence.

○ ○ ○

He stares straight ahead while she undoes the buckle of his belt and slides his pants down. She runs her hands under his shirt, across his stomach and chest. He pulls his pants even lower and out pops his penis. She surprises him—putting her lips on his, kissing him, easing her tongue into his mouth. His body tenses the way a cat stiffens when it is being carried somewhere it does not want to go. She takes pity and pulls away, takes his penis in her hand.

He is in her mouth. It is an unusually warm day and she is sweating. Perspiration trickles through her eyelashes and a drop or two seeps into her closed eyes. She is leaning over him, supporting most of her weight on one arm. The arm starts to tire; soon her jawbone begins to weary and sweat curls down her neck.

She thinks it's rather like bicycling—specific rhythms and some fatigue, similar to when she climbs hills. Also like bicycling, the physical discomfort is not enough to make her want to stop. He is breathing hard. She often hears herself gasping like that after a particularly difficult ascent. When he comes, she wonders whether he considers what they are doing an act of intimacy. Or not.

o o o

Their games are not remarkable. They employ the usual moves. Sometimes one of them tries a strategy they have read about, the Amar Gambit or the Cunningham Variation, but this presents a new set of difficulties they are not proficient enough to handle.

In between moves, she sometimes catches him gazing at her breasts, which causes her to think about the circumstances of their lives, distracting her from the game.

Flies flit about, landing on tables, or the mouths of coffee cups. The door bangs periodically, and someone who's just entered, a Matt or a Jim, an Ann or a Mrs. Smith either says hello to them, or doesn't. They always look up when they hear the door, startled out of their reverie, or contemplation of the chessboard.

She likes how he holds his hands while he thinks, clasped together, with the fingers interlocking, like some people pray and others do nothing.

o o o

Inside her house, the woman does the usual: bathes, eats and cleans things. She hauls garbage out to the composter, and feeds the animals. Some would say this is a dull and lonely life, but the woman doesn't think so. She sometimes considers the alternative, and it is not pleasant. She could move to a city a couple of hours away, pay too much rent for a ramshackle apartment in a rundown neighborhood, where she would dash up the steps, her key clenched and protruding from her fingers, poised to slip into the lock and let her into what she would hope would be two rooms of relative safety. While walking home from work, she could watch the monied pile out of limousines and head for the champagne bar at the Opera. Better to stay put, she thinks, where there are long, uninterrupted bike rides, and the beauty of the countryside, where the burnt oranges, burnished golds and deep greens await.

○ ○ ○

The woman hears the dreaded sound of air rushing out of a tube, feels her rear tire going flat and dismounts. Not a problem, she thinks. She spins the tire to pull out the object that punctured it, but there is nothing. She could have run over a rock, yet she cannot recall doing this—but sometimes a sharp piece of gravel is enough to cause a pinch in the tube. She takes the pump from her bike and reinflates the tire, but it will no longer hold air. The woman sighs; it is already misty and looks like it could rain. She pulls out her tools from the small bag fastened just below the bicycle seat, and reaches into the bag for a new tube. There aren't any. She digs through it frantically. Angry at herself for forgetting to replace it, she resigns herself to a very long walk.

A mile or so down the road she notices the enclosure and steel fence that contained the sheep. She hasn't looked for the animal in quite a long time. As she approaches the dwelling she cannot help but check. Nothing. The woman is quite startled by this discovery and is not sure why. As she is about to pass the structure she sees movement and stops. Deep within the pen is another sheep, large and black. The woman lays her bike on the road and goes over to the fence. It is a ram whose horns have been removed. It lingers at the back of the pen. Several moments earlier she'd felt a few drops of rain on her arms and several more drops have just fallen. She moves away from the structure and resumes walking her bike. What could have happened to the other? A rancher told her that sheep are prone to many fatal diseases— or it may have been sold at auction, like many of the animals in the area are.

She misses it in a vague, inexplicable way.

The woman thinks about movement, how protected and autonomous she feels on her bicycle, and how different it is on foot, where she is caught-up, vulnerable putting one foot in front of the other as rain drips from a slate gray sky.

Confessions of a Noun

THE ROOM IS perfect, slowly deteriorating, small as it should be, stains on the walls, a mirror defaced and beginning to tarnish. The cheese on the table smelling like cheese.

His novel written here. Her book of poems. A gray sky as if you'd planned it. A brief respite from walking, the restlessness temporarily gone out of your body. The cobblestone streets confusing—more real in the color photographs in oversized books.

It begins to rain as it should do while you sit at the writing table. Her novels. His poems. Their writing done in little rooms all over the city.

Your pen in your hand, your idea in your head. Your hand that will not move the pen. Your brain that will not hold a thought. Your ideas that abstract into images, things you'd be better off not thinking, followed by an unusual bird seen while walking near the river, the waiter you encounter daily who always fails to recognize you. Where is your imagination when you need it?

Appropriately it begins to rain harder and the sky darkens as if orchestrated. And as befitting you hear through the open window rapid footsteps on the cobblestones and wonder if you will ever meet any of the persons they belong to, and if you do, if you will fall in love with one of them and it will turn out badly, and if so, if you will afterwards transcribe them, or it, transfigured, of course, so they will be unrecognizable to themselves, and it as well, because understandably, they would have another it, as may well you when you are finished, this you with two hands and a pen in a rented room in the rain.

Conceptions

SAY IT IS 1972 and you are a beauty queen from the suburbs with bleached-blonde hair. Say you come from a poor background, but have aspirations.

Say you are a man, a bored man, a man who pursues pleasure.

Say you meet the man who pursues pleasure and he is pleased you are a beauty queen. Say you realize the man has a little money, more money than your male contemporaries who are young and just starting out. Say this fact is appealing.

Say you are feeling old and useless, and that sex with a beauty queen will make you feel young and virile (never mind the cliché).

Say sexual relations don't interest you much per se, but your mother always told you that if you let the man you are making love to believe he is throwing you into previously unreachable throes of ecstasy, the man will, afterward, always do what you ask—especially since you are a beauty queen. Say the feminist movement has just begun, but you decide that the media is right— feminism is for lesbians, and women not as beautiful as yourself.

Say you sometimes worry that the beauty queen is only having sexual relations with you to get your money so she can help her parents move out of their tiny apartment. Say you confront her with your fears, she bursts into tears, and you become all aquiver with emotion at such a perfect example of fragile womanhood. Say this vision of the beauty queen, vulnerable and weeping, stimulates your gender conceptions of women being weak and inferior to such an extent that you propose.

Say that after you are married your husband is always after you to make love to him, which you no longer find necessary. Say that you continually catch him staring at you, admiring your beauty, and you resent this, as it is the only thing about you which seems to hold his interest. Say in order to get him to leave you alone you tell him you've become a feminist. You don't really know what being a feminist entails as you don't read books on the subject; instead you order him around, make him wash dishes, prepare meals, and do laundry—while you get a job in middle-management.

Say that after you marry, your spouse has somehow gotten you to pay off all her debts, talks you into loaning money to her parents so they can move out of their tiny apartment. Say instead of the sweet, feminine personage you knew before the nuptials, this stranger smirks, and the words "community property" frequently come from her mouth.

Say you end up having infrequent sex with your spouse, just enough to keep him desiring you, and then you do what your friends suggest—neglect to use birth control. "Men will have a harder time leaving when children are involved."

Say you find yourself with two sulky children and a hostile spouse, deep in debt and without much equity in your home. Say you now find the beauty queen quite ugly. Say you scratch your head, unable to believe this is where you are, that this is what your life has become.

Say you are angry. You were a beauty queen and have ended up married to a man you are contemptuous of, a man, who, in the end, wanted only your surface. Not only this, but you are also deep in debt, without much equity in your home. Say you comfort yourself with the fantasy of having stuck to your goal of marrying a doctor, a lawyer, or a dentist, for you were a beauty queen and deserve a large Mercedes, a swimming pool, to dress in silk clothes.

Say you feel the need to grasp at something: a drink, a pill, another, a straw.

Zoo

It occurs to you that the only people you've spoken to in weeks are the clerks at the hotel, who are not friendly. You find yourself loitering in shops, engaging in long conversations with salespeople the way lonely people do.

You walk the streets of London, can't help but glance at your reflection in windows. Your face looks older, sad.

When you return to the hotel you look to the desk clerk, hoping he'll hand you a letter from your lover. There are often letters from your lover. His letters are energetic and witty in a way he is not; you take this to mean he likes you more when you are out of the country. You reached a plateau in your relationship long ago, have become a habit with one another which is, for the most part, pleasant.

In the final paragraph of the letter your lover requests you look up a friend of his. Enclosed is the man's photograph and telephone number. You don't want to meet his friend; you've gotten used to not speaking.

You go up to your room and after you sit on the bed, watching a woman in the apartment building next door share an early supper with her cat, make the call. The man is pleasant and amusing over the phone and you find yourself looking forward to seeing him—although you think it odd he wants to meet near the monkeys at the London Zoo.

Armed with a map they hand out at the entrance you race around the paths, trying to find the locale of the primates. You're going to be late; it takes so long to get through the queues in this country. You find the creatures and try to compose yourself, surrounded by a horde of English school children staring solemnly into the cages. The monkeys, like all animals in zoos, look lethargic and depressed. You pull the man's photograph from your purse and try to locate its correspondent.

Someone embraces you. You jump, saying as politely as you can, as the English insist on politeness, that this individual grappling with you has obviously made a mistake. But the man smiles and says your name. He turns to look at the monkeys, says there used to be more, but they've hidden away the ones that masturbate. He speculates sadly that they've probably sold them for research.

He asks if you'd like some tea. There's a tearoom over by the elephants, and the tea isn't bad. While you walk the man asks about your life in The States, what you've been doing in London, what plays you've seen. He talks so continuously you do not have to resort to your lover as a conversation topic. You're puzzled as to why your lover sent you such an out-of-date picture of the man. The individual in the photograph is middle-aged, rather robust, while the man speaking to you is thin and walks as if he is in pain.

The man wants to sit outdoors and watch the elephants, so he brings your tea back to a bench. It is too hot for you to drink and the plastic cup burns your hands. You observe an elephant take a log in its trunk and add it to another pile of logs. When the elephant moves all the logs from one pile to another, people clap.

You've run out of things to say. Awkward pauses are occurring and soon you're talking about your lover. You spend several minutes agreeing what an interesting and accomplished person your lover is.

The man looks at you with pity, leans forward, touches your hair and invites you to sleep with him. He knows your relationship with your lover will never be the way you want it; you can get revenge for the years of your life he's taken. The man swishes his tea around in his cup, stares into it, says quietly that he's ill, quite ill. If you have sex with him, you'll become ill—and can in turn kill your lover. Wouldn't you like that? What's your life worth anyway?

He stops staring at the tea, looks into your face, pronounces in a pragmatic tone that your years of attractiveness are past. . . You wouldn't even have to actually do it—although the two of you would probably both enjoy a good fuck. You can bite his ear and draw blood. You can stay on the bench. He's leaning toward you, two fingers behind his earlobe, offering it.

You discover you're in Bloomsbury, no longer able to run; you've nearly been hit by a Rolls and a black cab. The English politely turn away as you stand doubled over in Russell Square, gasping for air, close to hyperventilation.

In the days that follow you walk around London not really seeing the art on yet another museum's walls, not actually tasting the fish and chips you pick at in the pub, not quite absorbing the books you read in Hyde Park. You wish you could approach someone and say please talk to me, but cannot bring yourself to.

Whenever you think of what the man said you become upset. What is your life worth? True, you have accomplished several objectives, enjoyed some small successes, but do they equal worth, something worthwhile? You can think of no reason, other than the fact that you haven't died of disease, or been killed, for you to be. You do your work. You believe your lover loves you, and you him; years go by.

You don't attach importance to the things the man spoke of—yet somehow your veneer of toughness has been stripped away by a sick man on a bench in a zoo.

The thought of going to see the crown jewels, or a cricket match, or going to a station to see about trains to somewhere exhausts you. The trip to the airline office to change your ticket to an earlier departure proves unsuccessful.

How did you end up here? A wrong turn in Regent's Park, a lack of posted signs. The London Zoo. There is no admission, and no queue today. You enter, watch polar bears eat fish, giraffes eat leaves, a snow leopard with mange. The elephant is moving its logs from one pile and placing them on another. People are pleased to see this. And here are the monkeys. Sad-looking creatures. You like to observe their paws, so like human hands. A monkey spits; you look at the yellowish gob on your chest, slowly lower yourself to the ground, hope no one notices you rolling on the grass.

Your lover makes a complicated meal to celebrate your return, afterward makes love to you with enthusiasm. You observe your lover finds it essential to see you in some former incarnation of yourself, and you, in turn, choose not to notice things about him. Easier that way.

Your lover comes home one night, gulps a beer and begins to cry. He's just read his friend's obituary in *The London Times*. He can't believe it. He hadn't known his friend was ill. Had you?

Relief

YOU'RE DRUNK, BUT probably shouldn't be. It is a weekday afternoon and you're in search of a bathroom. As you arrive at a door saying Ladies, a woman shouts *run, run.*

At my age you run and it often doesn't do any good. She has followed you inside, is in the adjacent stall. Your silence is accentuated by the sound of two bladders being relieved.

What people confide during the holidays rarely startles or surprises—more strangers engage you in conversation at this time of year, and you are aware of more people intoxicated, or otherwise self-medicated.

June Allyson is very brave. . .doing those diaper commercials. You agree what a courageous and public-spirited person June Allyson is, although it requires some restraint to keep from mentioning June Allyson's inevitable payment.

June Allyson has always been a down-to-earth type of person. While lathering your hands you try and recall who June Allyson was, but are unable to, although you know she had something to do with Hollywood's Golden Age. It occurs to you, while you brush your hair out of your eyes, that the woman with the unreliable bladder might be inebriated too. *June Allyson was Burt*

Reynolds' only real love. You haven't thought of Burt Reynolds for a long time, in fact never do.

Your mind is not as clear as it could be, but you believe the woman is referring to the late Dinah Shore.

If you smooth your clothing you will probably have a more sober appearance, so you watch your reflection, tug at your dress and pull up your tights. *Enjoy it while you can.*

The door swings shut. Was that a warning, or has something else made you uneasy, frightened and unwilling to go back out there?

Heirloom

BEFORE THE WAR this mansion belonged to my family, who are Prussian in origin and consisted of many officers, but oddly, only one man of letters. Most of the original architecture has been kept intact—the parquet floors, the mahogany stairways, the chandeliers—even the colors, muted maroons, beiges and greens are the original decorator's tones. The servants rooms were up that stairway.

Through this door was the dining room. The dining table could seat thirty around it, and often did. Now it is used as a conference table. Just last week while passing this room I overheard a group speaking of our Kurt Richter. It became known that Richter was arrested as a Stasi agent after reunification. One of the participants asked if this had done anything to tarnish his reputation. But he was not harmed at all, in fact he is currently directing the summer season of Wägner. A penance, perhaps?

On this wall are photographs of many of the illustrious guests, taken some years ago. Let me open the drapes to show you the view. This district is named for that lake you're looking at. Our property went down the hill to its shore. At this time of year the lake is always filled with rowboats, motorboats, dinghies, and the ferry crosses several times a day. It is deceptively windy on the water—that is why the passengers are shouting and hang onto their hats. From now until the middle of September there will be picnicking on these shores. We had a very hard winter and people can't get enough of this blue sky and early summer weather.

Those on the grounds just below the window are the current residents. They hail from many places, but mostly other parts of Germany, Austria, the Czech Republic, France, and a few are from the United States. They stay between two weeks to six months. All are poets, writers, or dramatists. They are taking their lunch now, which is why they sit on the grass, smoking, writing letters, or are sharing food and conversation at the outdoor tables. Watch them for a time. Notice how they all glance across the water at that knoll. You see, long ago on a damp, foggy, November afternoon, a couple was seen there, cavorting and sipping brandy from a flask. A servant was sent out to inquire after their business, about which they were vague. The servant noted the man and woman joyfully embraced and spoke to one another in animated tones. The couple bade the servant to leave them, and they went down to the base of the knoll, which is protected from sight. The man, believing himself a failed dramatist, novelist and poet, pulled a gun from a wicker basket they'd brought with them, put it to the breast of his female companion who was suffering from an incurable illness and fired. He then put the gun into his mouth and fired again. Their remains were found doubled over in a pre-rigormortic state an hour or so later by a man on his way to a boating expedition. Suicide Notes which gave their identities were found in each of their pockets, and explained that neither could bear the pain any more, hers stemming from her ill-

143

ness, and his from the state the artist endures when 'his art no longer comforts him, when the artist's heart outlives his art.' Their graves lie under the linden trees at the top of the hill, for they insisted on being buried side by side, although the woman was married to someone else; as for the man, Heinrich von Kleist, romantic love and the passion for death were forever one.

All who come here soon learn of the story, and although the human mind does not retain a great deal of what it takes in, those in residence do not forget Kleist's final words, for afterward they are less self-assured, less buoyant. It may not be the next day, or the day after, or the day after that, but eventually our residents begin looking up from their work to the knoll, surreptitious glances, and no matter how sophisticated, no matter how hard they try to stop, all are unable to keep from doing so. As time passes uncertainty begins to flicker within them, and gradually, in imperceptible stages, it becomes their bane. I come to this window day after day to observe those covert glances—my comfort, my solace.

Negation

SHE GOES TO college, majors in art and becomes a sculptor. In only two years following graduation she has had a solo exhibit in an up-and-coming gallery, and received good notices in two group shows. At around this time she meets a law student who talks of his plans and ambitions after graduation. *Marry me*, he says, *we will have a nice life.* It never occurs to the woman to turn down a nice-looking man poised for success. In 1958 it doesn't occur to any woman she knows.

After graduation the man's career does not rise as quickly as either of them had hoped, and the woman is forced to take a job typing. When she gets home from work she pays the baby-sitter and attends to her baby daughters, who are usually cranky and fussy. When her husband comes home he drinks highballs and complains about his life. In a corner of the flat sit inanimate bundles of clay, but after one of her daughters tries to eat the clay, the woman throws it into a nearby dumpster.

The woman's husband finally gets a job with a good Manhattan firm, but it is competitive and he must work weekends and most evenings to stay on top of things. He is befuddled by his daughters: on Sunday afternoons during autumn he takes them to Central Park and tries to show them how to throw a football, and in springtime how to hit a baseball. The girls are quiet and sulky during the instruction, which only holds their attention for ten or so minutes.

The eldest girl develops an interest in ballet and is given lessons. Her younger sister is encouraged to take up the piano. The eldest girl becomes rather good and has a solo as the Sugar Plum Fairy in *The Nutcracker*. Several weeks before the performance the woman begins commenting to her daughter: *your hair is too stringy, perhaps we should have it cut before you go onstage;* or: *Stand up straight, don't they teach you poise and posture at that school?* And after attending a dress rehearsal her mother says wistfully: *so many of the girls in the production are so lissome and beautiful.* When the girl gets onstage she executes the steps competently but lacks charisma and confidence. The following day the girl's teacher calls her mother and says she just doesn't understand, she was delightful to watch in the preceding months. The woman says coldly that perhaps her daughter isn't cut out for performance and would be better off just dancing for exercise, and soon after, the girl quits ballet.

At thirteen the woman's eldest girl again tries the performing arts. This time she begins acting lessons, her teachers believe she shows promise and she is cast in the part of Amy in a dramatization of *Little Women*. The girl is careful not to talk about the upcoming performance, but while putting the girl's laundry away her mother discovers her costume in the closet. *Put it on* she commands when the girl arrives home from school. The girl complies and her mother scrutinizes her, frowning. Perhaps there is still time for the girl to lose five pounds before opening night, or maybe the wardrobe person could let the costume out several inches around the hips. The girl gives up acting after the show's closing night.

The woman's youngest daughter has always been distant from her family and impervious to her mother's barbs, so she is more or less ignored by her mother and the rest of her family.

In the early 1970s there is a real estate boom and the family buys a large house on Long Island. The man commutes into the city most days, and also takes a second job teaching a class at NYU.

A short time later the woman tells her husband that if he continues banging his students she will take him for everything he has.

The girls go off to college and the woman decides to resume sculpting, clearing out her oldest daughter's bedroom, filling it with clay, and installing a skylight. She enrolls in an advanced class at a community college to find motivation to begin work. The class is filled with women like herself, housewives with grown children. These women sculpt pots and cows, have never heard of Giacometti or Louise Nevelson.

The oldest girl drops out of school several times, and is hospitalized with an eating disorder. The youngest girl also drops out of college—to play keyboards in an all woman punk band who call themselves the Avenging Angels. She wears a safety pin through her nose, and is involved with an older woman who goes by the name of Butch.

The woman wants to work hard on her sculpture, goes to

galleries, reads art magazines, but every time she confronts a wedge of bronze or hunk of clay she is paralyzed. A year later she enrolls in a drawing class in the city, hoping that some of her sketches might translate into interesting sculptures. These drawings are more successful, and the instructor often praises them during critiques. Some of the younger women in the class come up and speak to her, admiring her work, and bluntly ask her about her life. After she gives them a vague chronology, they no longer come around, and once, when she sees several of them in the small quad, in their army fatigues, smoking clove cigarettes, she overhears one of them say, *there goes the Stepford Wife.*

One morning the woman receives a note from her oldest daughter saying the daughter's therapist recommends that she have no contact with her mother for ten years, after which they can meet and the daughter will inform her, by mail, after she and her therapist assess the meeting, if she wishes to reestablish contact.

The woman finally makes a friend. There are many things she doesn't like about the friend—she dresses too young for her age, unwittingly flirts with gay waiters when they lunch in restaurants, and uses the word lay when she should use lie. Nonetheless, when the woman looks in her appointment book and remembers she will see _____ during the coming week, she feels happier. The woman and her husband come and go and do not make one another account for their time. Sometimes when her husband is in the house she looks up, startled by how ugly he has become, attributes it to his drinking.

She and her friend often sit on her back porch and have tea.

Her friend likes to visit because she feels like she is on vacation when she goes to the woman's big, beautiful house that overlooks the water. They are careful not to talk about husbands or children, but one afternoon her friend asks about her daughters, after revealing that her son has decided to marry a simpering girl who is rather unstable and he cannot be talked out of it. The woman confesses her daughters' shortcomings to her friend. She puts her feet up on a wicker chair, looks out at the Long Island Sound and takes a sip of iced tea. She begins thinking, momentarily forgets anyone is there and murmurs, *a disappointment, yes.*

Routine

A MAN THROWS a boy headfirst down the stairs of a cheap boardinghouse. The boy lies in a heap at the bottom. As soon as he stirs, the man claps his hands, two terse claps, and the boy crawls up several stairs until he is oriented enough to clasp the banister and pull his way to the top.

Again the man says, taking the boy in his arms and hurling him like a caber in the Scottish Games. When the boy hits the floor tears spring to his eyes. *None of that* the man admonishes, surveying him from the second floor.

As the boy climbs the stairs for the third time a swelling begins to grow on his shin and a gash on his elbow leaves little drops of blood on the mahogany. This time the man grasps the boy with one arm around his shoulders, the other under the backs of his knees, and looks as if he is going to now fling him backfirst. But the landlady comes out of a second floor room and tells them that the session is over, they're making too much noise—however, would the man care for a whiskey? The man puts the boy down, says he would indeed and the two disappear behind a heavy wooden door. The boy sits at the top of the stairs, rubbing his wounds.

The boy becomes known as Buster Keaton, so called because Harry Houdini admiringly tells his father that the boy can take a real "buster" when the boy and man perform their routine.

The man becomes bitter, resentful of his son's talent, of his son's ability to consistently upstage him, and devises ways to steal a great deal of the boy's money. These schemes, though, rarely need to be acted upon, for the boy, reasoning that his father is, after all, his father, gives it to him willingly.

Cri de Coeur

A WOMAN DECIDES to start her own business. She works diligently and determinedly at it. During the first several years her business grows and she receives many compliments for her hard work, her ingenuity.

Several more years pass and the woman continues to work as hard, but her business does not grow as it once did. After another year, the woman is forced to face the fact that no matter how much she does, her business is stymied. She complains to her colleagues who tell her she should be glad she still has a business at all, pointing out a number of peers whose enterprises have failed in recent years. A business advisor reiterates that most of the population is slipping backward financially, and since what she sells is not absolutely essential for survival, many no longer buy it.

The woman redoubles her efforts, puts in longer hours, makes more phone calls, sends more faxes, and takes less of a salary in order to pay for more advertising. Most of the letters and faxes are never responded to, the recipients, hostile and frustrated with their jobs, toss them onto desk piles where they sit for several months and are eventually thrown into the garbage. The advertising campaign has little effect.

Potential investors feel her wares are not generic enough to induce them to take such a risk, so the infusion of money which would take her business to another level is not forthcoming.

The woman does not know what to do. She could sign the necessary papers, liquidate her assets and take a job with a large firm that produces uninteresting products, but she likes being her own boss, having to answer only to herself, working with her unique wares.

As the laws become more stringent, she finds she is paying more taxes, that more forms need to be filed, that she is spending more of her work time speaking to bureaucrats, or on hold, listening to dead air or irritating music.

The woman notices she feels increasingly tired, hears that many people are feeling this way, but this is not much comfort. She begins to procrastinate about making calls or responding to letters, and spends less and less time concerned with her business and ways to make it prosper. She finds herself staring out of her office window admiring the color of the grass in the nearby park.

She thinks about her dilemma: if she continues to put the ultimate care and energy into her business she will end up feeling thwarted, frustrated and hurt that the population takes so little interest in her merchandise. If she should take a more casual approach, she'd feel guilty, like she was letting herself down, exhibiting self-destructive behavior.

The woman makes more time for her other interests, but finds that the films she attends are formulaic and empty, the classical music concerts pedestrian and predictable, consisting of done-to-death pieces—Mozart, Mozart, Mozart.

In an attempt to create a more fulfilling life for herself, the woman begins to go out to places filled with people, hoping that some of the people in the places might be men, and one of these men might be someone she could care about. Her plan is successful to the degree that she does happen upon men, and several of these men are pleasant and interesting. Some of them are even interesting enough to take to bed.

She becomes involved with one of the men. However, as the year's end approaches, it becomes apparent that the man does not have sufficient interest in her to form a relationship of consequence. What he does seem interested in is arriving at her apartment with a pair of handcuffs, requesting that she fasten him to her bed, straddle him, and rock up and down on his erect penis. After these encounters, the foremost thing in the man's mind is having her go into great detail about his sexual effect on her.

The woman stops having relations with the man, as she does not want to leave herself open to caring for someone who is only interested in handcuffs and objectification.

She decides to re-establish her social life, get back in touch with her old circle of friends. But she finds them much changed: they hold their mouths tightly, their sense of humor has vanished. They constantly complain about their spouses or children, about how hard they have to work for an inequitable amount of money. They have taken to scorning others in their circle—for their lack of talent, for their wrong-headed ideas. The woman's old crowd barely has time to see her. Their new social life is centered on deriding one another in internet discussion groups night after night.

The woman wakes and remembers it is Tuesday. She sees from the clock that she's overslept, probably turned the radio off during the first strains of music. She congratulates herself on getting through Monday, however, she makes no move to get out of bed, finds it quite pleasant just to lie there.

She notes that the late morning light in her bedroom is very pretty. She'd never noticed this, indeed, she probably hadn't been in bed at such a late hour before. As she is disinclined to get up, she changes the radio dial now and again, listens to people call in to a talk show to express their opinion about the guilt or innocence of the defendant in an infamous murder trial. The woman is puzzled by what motivates them; their opinion will not affect the verdict in the least. And the ensuing callers do not pay any attention to what has been said, are only concerned with having their opinion go out on a station with a strong broadcasting signal.

An hour or so later a health-and-nutrition physician comes on the air informing the public that if they would only consume a vegan, fat-free diet, this to be followed by a weekly colonic wash, they would be filled with dynamism and positive thoughts, would almost assuredly recapture their fascination with living. This causes the woman to wonder if the entire country is rife with individuals spending Tuesday in bed, debating to themselves whether or not they have any interest in recapturing much of anything. She likens the phenomenon to a huge herd of animals rushing toward something, not certain as to why, like a genetic reflex—and after a time some drop away. After more time passes still more fall away. She thinks of the hundreds of thousands who have fallen away all over the country, inert with their radios droning on and on and on.

As the day progresses she notes that language ceases to sound like language. It becomes noises, sounds in various timbres, and primitive squawks. This transformation proves hypnotic, and takes her to a place deep in her mind, a place rather dark, but sometimes less so, and with varying degrees of mental comfort.

A Difficult Course

WE GASP UP hills and barrel down their descents. For us the utmost experience is striking the balance of to-the-limit speed and staying upright, cornering with enough aggression to keep close to the axis of a turn, yet with enough control not to land in a heap, bloody, with road burn, or an even more severe injury and out of the race.

On some of the less arduous sections of the course we catch a glimpse of terraced land crowded with thick green vines, on which are clustered either red or pale green grapes. The harvest is still a couple of months away. That is not important. What matters is timing it so when one of the volunteers hands off a water bottle I don't lose too many seconds reaching for it.

I pour some water over my head so it will seep through the air holes of my helmet and bring me some relief.

I've been gaining ground steadily, have passed several people on the ascents, know from their body language that they have given up; their shoulders sag as they shift into a lower gear and settle for just making it to the finish line. There are only about fifteen miles left, and considering how unexpectedly hot it is for late morning, I do not feel all that bad. The blue spots I occasionally see after blinking are a result of mild dehydration, but if I can get a bit more water from someone in the next group of spectators, I should be able to get off the course without cramping.

There aren't many other cyclists around this late in the race to draft from. The teams have gone ahead, supporting one another so they will have a strong overall finish, and at this stage the individual riders are scattered all over the course.

Armed with another bottle of cold water offered up by an onlooker, I'm hitting one of those interludes where I feel removed from my body. Two strong legs encased in bike shorts are turning pedals at a good pace. All *I* am responsible for is not making mistakes cornering.

Further ahead is a row of pine trees and I'm looking forward to the interlude in their shade. It seems like a grotto, since my eyes take a long time to adjust behind the goggles. It's cool and peaceful. I ride so much the bicycle seems like an extension of my body and in this shade I could just as well not be bicycling, although I know I am.

o o o

A marker says four miles to go. The course is nearly devoid of spectators now. The tourists have probably wanted to get out of the sun, get into air-conditioned cars and go wine tasting. Maybe there will be a few left to give polite applause at the finish line.

With less than a mile left I see another woman on the course, am puzzled that she wasn't in sight before, assume she was having a great ride, perhaps drafting from a team or team member, then slowed—maybe from cramping, maybe from heat exhaustion.

I'm determined to catch her. It is hard to tell how old she is with her hair tucked under her helmet and goggles covering her eyes, but I have to assume that she is in my division. Will she allow me to pass her, or will we play sprint-and-pursuit?

I am beginning to hurt. I might throw up. If I keep pushing this hard I'll lose seconds vomiting. As I glance over my shoulder I see the woman will not fall back, is going to compete. I was told before getting on the course that there would be one last hill, then an easy finish. Since I am smaller than this woman, I'll go all-out to do a good climb, so she, who is larger, can't use her weight and momentum to beat me on the descent.

Once I stand and begin to really work, I can see her hesitate momentarily. I'll resist the temptation to glance back to check if she has risen out of the saddle to do a proper climb. On the downhill I tuck down to compound my speed, lessen the wind-resistance and remember something I heard yesterday from two of the male racers at the hotel: there was supposed to be a competitor in the women's division that something terrible had happened to. A bad crash I immediately assumed, but they had both shaken their heads *no*—something else, nothing to do with cycling. One of them looked at me, slightly frowning, as if this gesture should tip me off to what it was. The first thing I thought was cancer, and then rape.

These are not the things you should think about while racing. I'm overtaken with the impulse to drop back and let the woman win, but it is impossible to know if this person behind me is the one something unspeakable had happened to. Why is it unspeakable?

Back on the flat I begin to think the whole thing was a hallu-cination, that no male racers had spoken to me. I can't tell if this is a sort of delirium brought on by fatigue and the heat.

The woman is fairly far behind, I doubt she can catch me and I'll just maintain a steady pace until the finish line.

o o o

I ride under a banner, some people applaud, and a man announces me and my number on a bull horn, the instrument distorting the sound so much that I do not recognize my own name. As soon as I dismount, my husband runs up and throws his arms around me. The sweat on my jersey leaves an oblong spot on his shirt. He hands me a liter of bottled water, takes my bike to the car, while I wait in the shade.

When all the results are tallied I am given a silver cup that has *Wine Country Half-Century 1998* on it, and under-neath this is inscribed: *Winner Ladies Open Division*. I shake a man's hand and say thank him. I take my trophy to where my husband is standing so he can hold it too. It isn't real silver.

On our way back to the hotel I put the passenger seat back and recline like a discarded rag doll. My husband is having a vicarious thrill, is very enthusiastic and proud and keeps talking. I should be proud too. I have ridden fifty miles before, not in such heat, but with some discomfort, certainly. As my husband speaks I think about how my instincts, the training from my life in various sports manifested themselves without my even think-ing about it—do everything you can to win. If someone comes along and beats you, well that sometimes happens, but do everything you can to not let anyone be better.

It suddenly seems silly, and a rush of embarrassment flares up inside me. Perhaps my mood will pass when we get back to the hotel and I've had a shower.

○ ○ ○

At each winery my husband manages to slip into the conversation that I've just won the Women's Open division of the Wine Country Half-Century. Sometimes the person pouring the wine, and those also standing at the tasting bar, are interested. Often after hearing the news the person manning the tasting bar is extra generous when pouring the various wines. After my husband has made the statement, those who overheard him take a furtive look at my body, especially my legs.

Perhaps it is the heat of the day or the extreme exertion from the race, but the alcohol isn't agreeing with me. My husband becomes more animated with each stop, or discovers a cabernet sauvignon to his liking. Inside the last tasting room he began to tell people I am going to be in the next Olympics.

At this present winery, I have decided not to go inside, remain in the shade at a picnic table under some wisteria. Sometimes my husband strikes me as extremely vulnerable and absurd. Instead of feeling love, I feel embarrassed for him as a person moving through his life and the world. At this moment I can't imagine ever sleeping with him again, although throughout our marriage we have made love fairly often.

161

Would anyone notice if I stretched out on this bench? It is tranquil, and I can hear them in the tasting room, talking loudly, the way people talk at a party.

My husband is determined to enjoy my victory, and under the influence of wine and afternoon sun wants to entertain the fantasy that I can make an Olympic team. Thirty-six-year-old women don't make these teams, especially if they were not world class athletes when younger. Still, perhaps he senses that this is one of the highlights of my life, our life—a silver-plated cup in a small race at a tourist destination.

Maybe I made a mistake marrying. I married late, had never really planned on being a wife, and wandering through this odd labyrinth of feelings causes me to reflect on what is wrong with me.

I am certain those male cyclists told me about that woman, but whether they were joking, or deliberately said something to upset me and my racing strategy, I'll never know. I can't help but speculate about what happened. For some reason I begin to think about a man with a knife, her fending the attacker off. The woman's arms being cut as she tried to protect her face and body, and the attacker's surprise at her bravery. How long did she endure what was nearly unbearable, and for how long after was she so disassociated from it that it didn't seem real?

After winning an athletic event a person is supposed to think: 'I am good, strong and I have mental fortitude.'

My husband comes out of the winery waving two bottles of wine he has purchased. On our way to the next winery he tells me about the nose on one of the cabernets he has just bought. I ask him if he would mind if he dropped me off at the inn where we are staying, so I could take a nap. He is disappointed—no one wants to go wine tasting by themselves, but he agrees; he can catch up with some of the people he's met at the last winery.

° ° °

Before dozing off I remember a man I saw at dinner last night. He was old and his face had hollows in it as if some of his teeth were missing. He was sitting with his elderly wife, apparently enjoying himself. I noticed that his left hand, the one not holding his fork, was shaking.

I do not want to be old and lose my teeth and have quivering extremities. When the inevitable happens will it be better to have won bicycle races, to be able to look back on that—or when frail not ever to have experienced athletic prowess? One day I will arrive at the future, the finish line, will know.

° ° °

Dinner at the inn that night is a four-course meal. My appetite has finally come back and the food is quite good. As he eats I look at my husband's forearm, spattered with sun freckles, and think I am feeling the tender feelings that I should. As the second course arrives, the proprietor brings over a bottle of California sparkling wine, saying *Compliments of the inn.* It is to congratulate me for winning the race, which my husband must have told him about while I was asleep. The proprietor pours it with self-conscious ceremony.

I've had enough—of drink, of food, of bicycle racing, of my husband and this inn. It sometimes feels like I've had enough of living too. I've been around long enough to get it, to get the picture. But of course I can't say this. Instead I raise my glass and tilt my head back. Instead I say thank you.

The Golden State

IF SHE DIDN'T stop traffic, she certainly slowed it down. The California Girl's long, blonde hair flew out behind her, her breasts bounced inside the black spandex jogbra and her slim, lightly muscled legs were barely covered by skimpy red running shorts. She was an icon health-and-fitness woman, right down to the sunglasses she wore while running.

There were two incongruities to this picture: the first was that it occurred not on the jogging path on Ocean Boulevard in Santa Monica, or on the wide streets of Beverly Hills, but on a two-lane highway in a small northern California town, on which traveled large pickup trucks driven by men in baseball hats, battered and broken down cars driven by university students, and the occasional luxury car with a mogul from the burgeoning wine industry behind its wheel. The second discrepancy was that as she ran she pushed a large stroller, built for two. It was this stroller, I believe, that kept male drivers in the trucks and cars from thrusting their heads out of windows or sunroofs and shouting *yeehaaaahh,* or *great tits, baby,* or *do you want to suck it?* The apparatus put her on a pedestal, encompassing the ideals of motherhood and physical perfection.

From my bench at the bus stop across the road I watched cars slow and speed up again after their drivers had gotten an eyeful of her body, and the presence of the stroller registered. Several days a week I waited for the number 63 after classes at the university.

On nice days I bicycled to school and en route home came face-to-face with the woman, who obeyed pedestrian traffic laws and ran facing automobiles and bicycles.

∘ ∘ ∘

Whether on my bike or at the bus stop, I'd slowly come out of the fog that overcame me whenever I was at the university. At eighteen I'd talked my parents, liberal and accommodating people, into allowing me to spend a great deal of my college fund traveling in Europe. The institution I eventually enrolled in was located in the area where I was living, and not expensive. The classes were not lecture halls, but interactive, meaning that the most bombastic or most emotionally needy students dominated the sessions. A typical example was someone who, after reading Blake's "The Mental Traveller" took control of the seminar, contemptuous of Blake's entire oeuvre saying that since Blake never had children he didn't know what he was talking about.

A regular in creative writing classes who'd apparently never read anyone besides Kurt Vonnegut and in the 70s, Carlos Castaneda, came to class reeking of marijuana and for the next several hours babbled whatever came into his head.

The professor of the short story was not interested in any other workings in a text but symbols, and made students search

166

for them, an Easter egg hunt for adults, and of course those who found the most received the top grade.

Since we were studying the arts they wanted us not to think so much as to *feel.* I couldn't fathom any particular reason to share my feelings with strangers, so sat there.

It was puzzling that only one of the professors knew and taught anything about postmodernism, and that no classes on Marx and Freud, two thinkers who certainly influenced the century, were offered. Before the huge budget cutbacks to state schools one of the librarians had ordered books on contemporary thought, culture and philosophy. A handful of us checked them out, read and discussed them in coffeehouses and inexpensive restaurants.

o o o

Whenever I saw the jogging woman I wondered what she did that allowed her to be out exercising daily at 1 p.m. Even if she were a homemaker, it was more than likely something would come up forcing her to be elsewhere, at least on occasion.

o o o

After graduation I found a challenging job with an arts organization. Although it wasn't lucrative, I liked what I was doing and worked my way up to associate director.

I had owned a car while in college, but it was old and I only drove it when absolutely necessary. After I got the job I decided to invest in a new car and my work took me to a different part of the county. I didn't see the jogging woman any longer, forgot about her and the image she presented.

∘ ∘ ∘

This area of northern California was once predominately farmland. Over the years more and more people relocated here as four hour commutes to well-paying jobs in the city and back no longer seemed unthinkable. Grapes became the dominant agriculture, and with them came attractive, well-designed wineries that served as tourist destinations. Three and four-star restaurants sprang up to accommodate the tourists' hunger.

The university changed its emphasis from liberal arts to business and raised its fees. Students who wore tie dye, sandals and had been enrolling in classes for ten years because they liked learning things were suddenly gone. People died. Others moved in.

As more and more gentrification occurred no one referred any longer to this place as the country, as in *I'm going up to the country* without the word wine preceding it, and the areas with vineyards had drunken people careening around in them every weekend.

∘ ∘ ∘

I, in turn, began to crumble. It was not anything that was noticeable as it was not a physical malady, and when I saw my friends I tried to be entertaining and enthusiastic.

I was in my 30s, numb and more-or-less uninterested in my existence, on bad days comforting myself with a quote from Schopenhauer: "Human existence must be a kind of error," reasoning that my attitude was just something that developed after being alive for a certain amount of time. I noticed Europeans did not come to this conclusion as readily, but many did here in the States.

A boyfriend decided I suffered from Seasonal Affective Disorder and during the particularly long rainy months began seeing a woman who was more affluent and cheerful. A man I dated for a short time afterward only wanted to get together one night a week—to have dinner, drink a bottle of our local wine, followed by sex, telling me that he was doing me a favor, for on the other six evenings he was leaving me time to get things done.

While visiting friends in another part of the state I found myself having sex on a park bench in Santa Monica with a man I'd had a crush on in college. He'd moved away to work for one of the studios, and I remember thinking that my naked buttocks were parallel to the horizon line of the Pacific Ocean as I straddled him, and whether or not this was of any particular importance.

Several trips back to Europe rekindled my zest for life, but when I returned so did my lassitude. Despite my persistent efforts to find employment in London or Paris, nothing materialized in either place that would have allowed me to support myself.

o o o

The arts organization I worked for gained in prestige and I was appointed executive director. With its prestige and my position came acquaintances I'd known for years who called me up and read their poetry over the phone while I was trying to work. Casual friends with whom I'd lost touch invited me out to dinner, and although the places we met were crowded and noisy, they pulled out stories or novel excerpts and decided to give a reading. That I only was able to hear a sentence or two now and again and told them so, did not stop them. *Just a few more pages*, they'd say.

Two burly, bearded painters of around fifty whom I'd met at a party crashed into my office one Wednesday afternoon sweating and out of breath. They were carrying half a dozen 6 x 5 foot canvases, oil paintings of groups of burly, bearded men dancing around a campfire wearing loincloths and antler headpieces. In the background more burly men in fringed buckskin pants beat drums in a forest. They lined the canvases up against one of the office walls and tried to insist I give them a show, saying if I didn't like these they had other paintings—beautiful landscapes of our county's green, rolling hills, dotted by Holstein cows with black-and-white markings.

I saw my social life shrink as the tenor of my friendships changed. Nearly everyone I knew wanted me to read something they had written, or view something they'd painted or photographed. When I did not react in the way they had fantasized, didn't give them exhibits, or recommend their work to publishers, they became, hostile, distant and stopped calling.

The advent of the internet made it possible for me to work out of my home and only go into the office once or twice a week.

Meetings usually took place after lunch and I came to discover after being twice late that one could not take the freeway in the early afternoon. It was built in the early 1960s and had never been expanded to accommodate the current population. Mangled cars, accompanied by tow trucks, highway patrol officers filling out reports and stopped traffic had become a daily scenario.

It was while taking one of the back streets to the meeting and passing the university that I saw the jogging woman. Her long hair still flew out behind her and she ran while pushing the stroller, looking exactly the same. I didn't pay much attention because I was thinking about the meeting, but when it concluded and I was having coffee with a co-worker, it occurred to me that the babies in the stroller would now be in junior high school and at least five feet tall.

o o o

I continued to see the woman jogging with the stroller when I occasionally passed the university. Sometimes I speculated that she must operate a day care center, taking the youngest infants out during her daily exercise, while a co-worker stayed with the older children. At other times I thought that when she discovered the stroller's protective properties and when her children grew too large, she placed dolls in it, or small dogs that stayed put. Since the stroller had a large canopy partially concealing what it contained and drivers passed by at speeds of around 45 mph or faster, it was entirely plausible that the stroller was empty.

Strange, I thought, that she should continue to run on the main thoroughfare. Many sub-divisions had sprung up around it and there was no need for her to do something aerobic with wide open lungs while simultaneously inhaling carbon monoxide and other automobile emissions. She could have taken the many meandering side streets named Zinfandel or Chardonnay, which were devoid of people and automobiles since most who resided there needed double incomes to pay the mortgage and had driven to work hours earlier.

○ ○ ○

The French have an expression, les croulants, meaning the crumbling ones, but it refers to aging, decrepitude and impeding death. This was not my problem, not yet, although the generation preceding mine was the first that had decided to resist getting older, to combat gravity's effects. It was especially true of those who lived on the west coast—to such an extent that men and women in their late twenties and thirties stood under bright lights and peered into mirrors, bemoaning each infinitesimal line. It was so insidious that it infiltrated the minds of those who were not shallow, vain or stupid. Life was not kind to most people and they wanted to look as if they had never suffered any of life's defeats.

Being in my body, in this skin, perhaps I didn't see myself the way others did. A friend of mine who also worked in the arts warned me that I should do something pretty soon—by which he meant marry and settle down. When I said there wasn't anyone I was interested in, he said I should settle for a Mister Not-

172

So-Bad because my eggs were getting old and would eventually rot, even if I was a vegetarian.

○ ○ ○

My greatest disillusionment working in the arts was the fact that many of the participants had the same approach to life and their work as businessmen and women—the only difference was that they made much less money. Not content to let their art propel their careers, they connived, manipulated and struggled for power with as much fervor and determination as anyone on a corporate ladder.

While alone in a café having dinner and waiting for my food, I saw an up-and-coming photographer enter through the glass doors. I waved and he came over to my table, asking if I wanted company, which I did. After the meal, he asked he if could show me some solarized prints, which were in a portfolio in his car. I liked him and accompanied him to the parking lot. Although it was quite cold he unzipped his fly and pulled out his penis, holding it in his right hand. It took me about a minute to process that a man I was walking next to was holding his penis on a cold December night while supposedly about to show me some photographs. I wondered if his intention was for me to take it in hand. *I have to go* I said, and without another word walked to where my car was parked. He hadn't followed me. As I drove away I wasn't frightened or angry because his gesture did not seem the least bit threatening. I was confused. Was it business, did he want my organization to give him a show—or was my loneliness so apparent that he trying to be helpful?

o o o

Get out of here, go to New York, my friends said. At one time those who worked for arts organizations, and writers and artists could move to New York, rent a reasonably priced apartment, meet those with similar interests, discuss art, philosophy, literature, go to readings, exhibits, theatre and so on. In recent years the only artists I knew who lived in New York City were ones who had lived there a long time, with controlled rent, or those with trust funds. Almost everyone of my acquaintance lived in Brooklyn or the Bronx and worked fifty hours or more per week, not on their art but at the jobs they needed to survive. They never got near a theatre because tickets were too expensive and what was staged was predictable and reliable—since rents were so high no theatre company could take risks on new, innovative productions.

When my friends arrived home they were so exhausted that many projects were put on indefinite hold. These were well-respected poets, writers and visual artists, with a history of publication or exhibits. They had received positive reviews, had been awarded grants, prizes and other signs of affirmation.

Another way people in the arts survived in New York was to marry a non-artist and attempt to be a nurturing housewife or househusband in between pursuing their careers. These arrangements did not usually last long, for those in the arts became too involved in their work, forgot about their domestic duties, frequently went out drinking and, or, had sex with those of similar

174

aesthetics—which resulted in their spouses throwing them out.

∘ ∘ ∘

You cannot drive down a main street in any of the small towns in this county without coming across a wine bar, and so this is where we were, a friend and myself, drinking merlot and trying to talk above the din. On a mirror behind the bar were this evening's wine specials, written in black felt pen, but we could see ourselves behind the print. *A terrible thing to happen to a girl* she said when we observed our images.

From our life in the margins and the wine county we exchanged several books. While my friend was reading the dust jacket of one of the titles, I thought about the jogging woman and wondered if she ran in the rain. It had been raining all day, had continued into the evening. My friend had just arrived from the gym, freshly showered, her hair still damp and her face flushed from jogging on a treadmill, becoming more so after she'd had some wine.

Did the jogging woman create the life she wanted, fighting to keep everything static, and given her appearance and routine, succeeding? It is not unusual here that many try to make time seize up. The leisure and financial security of being able to repeat activities over and over again is considered the good life, while having any sort of victory in staving off time and change is regarded as a triumph. People sometimes refer to this place as God's country, because of the hills, vineyards and the Pacific ocean only twenty minutes away, but with God in absentia—a heaven with wine bars lit to make everyone appear just a little more attractive, laughing and happy voices intermingled with soft jazz, wine bottles lined up, and the clientele in reasonably good health, but not much else.

The following morning I woke up fuzzy-headed but made myself a pot of coffee, went to the computer and began working. I did several hours of good, solid work which I should have been pleased about, but instead it was just a series of tasks I was able to cross off the "to do" list.

I decided to run my errands in the early afternoon and deliberately went past the university. There she was so predictably in the distance, running past the university's main entrance. After all these years I couldn't decide if I found her compelling or annoying as she raced west, her brain and body saturated with endorphins, as if her salvation was held within their chemical components.

I watched for several seconds until she became a speck of red-and-black spandex, moving in the bike lane in between a line of cars and a row of eucalyptus trees, then turned my attention to the road as traffic suddenly became dense and the driver ahead of me decided to repeatedly hit the accelerator then jam on his brakes—for no apparent reason.

Holiday

SHE RESOLVES TO be cheerful, but queues up a CD of Bach sonatas, which would make the most buoyant person mournful. Sonata #4 drifts into the bathroom as she stands putting on makeup. When she finishes, fatigue creeps into her body, her brain. She's only been awake for an hour, so will not allow herself to be tired. The woman applies a finishing touch of lipstick. She is fairly certain wearing makeup makes it easier to face the world.

The woman drives to her office to finish up some pre-holiday details. She dials information for a telephone number. The information operator gives her the wrong one—for a meat packing plant in Mississippi. When she calls again to request the charge be removed, it seems to cause a great deal of confusion and annoyance on the part of the present operator. At the end of the discussion she resigns herself to the probability that the charge will appear on her statement—at least once.

She must also send some information to a company, and calls the receptionist for the e-mail address and fax number. The e-mail bounces almost immediately, and after she writes out a fax, the company's fax machine rings and rings without making any connection. When she calls to recheck the number, there is a recorded message saying the office will reopen on January 3rd.

The woman remembers a time, not all that long ago, when the numbers she requested were correct, when packages arrived at their appropriate destinations, and when telephone calls, faxes and other communications elicited responses.

o o o

It is a well-established fact that people become more psychologically unbalanced at this time of year and her car is almost hit by several sport utility vehicles on her way downtown.

In several shops the woman buys last-minute gifts and stands in line to have them wrapped. She hopes they are the right books, that it is the ultimate sweater, and if not, that these items will not be completely useless or offensive to the recipients.

At the market while buying the usual holiday accoutrements, sweets and fattening food, a store clerk crashes a dolly loaded with cases of wine into her ankle. He responds with an indifferent *sorry*, and leaves her hopping toward the breads.

Out in the parking lot she finds she is blocked in by someone who is double-parked, dumps her groceries in the backseat and honks the horn. Customers glare at her as they enter the store. No one comes to move the car, so while honking and waiting, the woman pulls a pear from one of the grocery bags and begins to eat. For the first part of the season she has found herself absently putting food into her mouth and now feels uncomfortably expanded, as if her body were a damp sponge.

A man in rotting clothing who has left a Salvation Army store-front crosses the parking lot swearing loudly: *Bastards. It's Christmas and they still won't give me a coat! They talk about* RULES. *Jesus never had any rules, only teachings.* The man sees her looking at him and shouts at her through the rolled up car window: *can't even have a drink with Christmas dinner at the shelter. No money, they treat you like a little kid.* He wanders off without even asking for change.

The pear isn't enough. Shortly after eating it she is more hungry than before. She would like to fill her stomach and sleep under a thick blanket until sometime in the new year.

○ ○ ○

That evening the woman's boyfriend calls and she can tell he's been drinking. He suggests they break up, but after talking non-stop for another fifteen minutes, says perhaps they should get married. She isn't sure if he is proposing, decides that is something she does not want to think about just now.

○ ○ ○

On Christmas the family decides to be hyper-convivial, which makes for a hysterical tension lying below their every move and word.

The woman has a hard time discerning if anyone likes the gifts she has gotten them—or not—if the oohs and aahs are imitation oohs and aahs.

Around the table some pick up the thread of an argument begun the year before, perhaps unconsciously, for they all know how to upset and annoy one another—or they just can't help themselves. A cousin seated next to the woman covertly discusses with another cousin how her father would have preferred a daughter like that—indicating with her knife a woman toward the head of the table, another cousin's second wife. She is thin, with hair curled by a curling iron, who smiles at everyone and seems to be eating only vegetables. The whispering cousin suddenly throws her knife onto her plate and leaves the table to go outside and smoke a cigarette.

At the other end of the table a nephew takes an entire platter of appetizers in one of his large hands, dishes mini-quiches onto his plate and monopolizes the conversation, saying things like it is wrong to stage a war and bomb innocent people to retain political power. He seems to think his superior mental powers have drawn him to this conclusion before anyone else.

An aunt rolls her eyes at a brother-in-law's tie adorned with hot air balloons, a gift, undoubtedly, from one of his children— while a father eats with rapid bites, hunched and concentrated on his plate, like someone is lurking behind his chair waiting to whisk away his meal if he were to pause.

They gather in the living room for the after-Christmas-dinner movie, a comedy that should offend no one. During the film, which doesn't hold the woman's interest, she reads a magazine article stating that aging is the result of damaged cells caused by free-radicals roaming loose in the body. Free-radicals are formed from unhealthy food, alcohol, pollution and other environmental factors. It explains that cells succumb to oxidation—the same process that causes wine to spoil, butter to turn rancid, paint to chip and peel away.

She can feel the blood pounding in her temples and wonders if her blood pressure has been raised by the Christmas food and the family—which seems like a meta-family she is now engulfed in without a self.

That night as the woman tries to sleep in a guest room, she lies awake hearing sounds she is unused to—doors slamming, wind blowing through wooden shutters, a toilet flushing in another part of the house.

In her worst moments she thinks all her life consists of is going from menstrual cycle to menstrual cycle—as when older it will be going from pension check to pension check. *Cheerful,* she admonishes herself and rolls over in the bed.

o o o

The following day she stops for breakfast on the road and indulges herself in an omelet, potatoes and lots of strong coffee. She feels depleted, weak. The smell of a grill, the flowered curtains and waitress uniforms are reassuring. She wonders if she and her boyfriend will continue. Ever since Thanksgiving their disagreements, sarcasms and hurt feelings have escalated to another level and lurk like phantoms behind their current conduct and words.

Back in the city she decides to run a few errands before returning to her apartment, which will be cold, since before leaving she turned the heat down to save money.

The people she encounters in the post office, in the store that sells high quality coffee and teas, at the shoe shop with a post-Christmas 50% off, are dazed, bewildered. There is a considerable lag time before they answer questions or ring cash registers.

When the woman arrives home, she turns up the heat, puts away her purchases and turns on the CD player. She forgot to remove the last disc so the familiar music once again floats through the apartment. It seems different today, wistful rather than melancholy.

She calls several people who remained in the city for the holiday. Some she leaves messages for, but those she speaks to are also distracted and unable to concentrate.

She has time on her hands and doesn't know what to do.

Everyone behaves as if they have been away for a long time, and have just returned, weary and blinking, from a vivid yet peculiar country.

She sits on the couch and imagines she must be comporting herself in the same way, but being in and of herself, ensconced in a body, inhabiting a brain—with cognition occurring and synapses firing, she cannot get far enough away from herself to know.

Perhaps those she saw over the last twenty-four hours had, in turn, scrutinized her—although she finds this somewhat unlikely, as most seemed to place their attention elsewhere. Nonetheless, she considers that they, too, were observing and deducing. If she made an impression, she speculates on its duration: a minute, longer? She wonders if the notion had gone beyond "relative," or "customer?"—and if the surveillance had gone deeper, did the thoughts run along the lines of: 'Here is someone I believe I know well because we are blood.' Or, 'This person appears demure—I do not need to prepare myself for unpleasantness and difficulty.' She reflects on the amount of time she might have existed in their consciousness, how long they had hovered about in hers.

As she sits on the couch halfway listening to a Bach sonata, she has the feeling she is now being watched. It could be the smug owner of a new telescope, a gift from the previous day, or it might be a thin man framed behind window panes. Someone could even be perceiving her as she is at this moment seeing herself—a small thing in a smallish room, an entity caught up in a prodigious and complex scheme she never agreed to be in, and which in spite of all the eyes and vocabularies, continues to elude them all.

Flesh and Blood

A PIANIST AND violinist hold the same note while looking critically at one another. The violinist fiddles with the instrument's tailpiece and the process is repeated.

People search for seats, their movements inadvertently become constricted, more unsure as they make their way from lobby to church.

The musicians, satisfied that their instruments are in tune, disappear through a side door while the last of the audience sidles in, searches for empty places in the pews.

Introduction and applause. The musicians reappear, briefly repeat their tuning, and we are told by the violinist that Charles Ives was the first American classical composer to shun the influence of the European masters in favor of American folk music and revivals, that his music is more romantic than some of the Romantics.

The violinist removes a navy blue bandana from his pocket, places it between his cheek and violin, and they begin Ives' *Sonata No. 3 for Violin and Piano, Op. 100.*

It is soon obvious that the violinist is dominating the performance, wants and has all eyes upon himself; the pianist, a young, serious-looking fellow from Julliard seems to have accepted his fate, is complicit in it.

Perspiration rolls down the violinist's face, his body moves with the music, eyes closed, and it is doubtful whether he is still aware he is before an audience. This Paganini-like trance could be an affectation to give the audience what he believes they desire—to observe a violinist looking mesmerized, sweating with intensity, before a church crowded with music aficionados on a Saturday afternoon.

The pianist is hunched over the keys and looks as if he would prefer to be in a practice room. He is as seemingly controlled as the violinist is passionate, but these personae could have been worked out during rehearsals.

The violinist has a small paunch, although he is what you would call a thin man, an odd observation to make during an opus. It is not clear if the violinist senses on any level that his body is being beheld and considered, and if so, if this makes him nervous, pleased, embarrassed.

Interspersed throughout the church are stained glass windows. Think of the labor and artistry involved in their production. It is possible that the workers who made the glass lost teeth, grew ill and died from a lifetime of exposure to the poisonous lead components.

Men sleep. Their heads loll to one side, hands loosely folded; some of these hands are marked with brown spots, some of these heads revealed through thin wisps. The companions of these men, wives presumably, nudge them gently if they seem to be in danger of snoring. These wives, many heavy and well-dressed, watch the musicians, absorb the music with eager, open faces. The other women, those in attendance with female friends, or with their daughters, are predominantly slender. Their daughters might be music students, given how their faces are focused with concentration. They're more delicate than their mothers, and it is frightening to think of what harm could come to them—and their mothers, how easily they could be robbed or beaten, or their legs forced open for a rape. Could some of these women even offer one effective punch, a good kick to ward off an attacker? Perhaps, aware of their apparent frailty, they have become proficient at martial arts, self-defense, carry mace in their purses, or on their persons.

It is odd to think of hearts, so many beating in one place at one time, and given the size of the audience, some must beat in unison. Does the man with blue eyes in the gray pinstripe suit have a heart pulsing in synch with the matron in beige linen? The hearts of the sleeping men may beat irregularly, the cause of their fatigue; it could be that their hardening ventricles, the enplaqued arteries are wearing out. Do the other hearts, belonging to those who appear so enraptured, subtly increase their beats and return to resting pulse rate according to the tempo of the music?

If looked at long enough fingers are strange things, pliant sticks with muscle memory, able to perform intricate movements to produce music in precisely the right way, at exactly the right time.

A sheath containing blood, bone and bile is a strange thing to have, is an odd vessel to go through life in, thinks one sullen inside its skin.

The musicians conclude the *adagio cantabile*, hold the final notes until they fade entirely from the church and there is a silent interval before some leap up to exit and others lumber up to deliver applause.

photo by Michelle Lyman

CYDNEY CHADWICK is the author of eight books and chapbooks of fictions and prose poems, the most recent of which is a novella, *Benched*, which was selected as a Critics Choice in the *Northern California Bohemian*. In 1997 she received a creative writing fellowship from the California Arts Council and 1998 won the New American Writing Series Award in fiction. A third generation Californian, she grew up in northern California—in Marin and Sonoma counties. She continues to live in Sonoma County.

COVER PHOTOGRAPHER Ben E. Watkins lives and works as a professional photographer in Boston, Massachusetts. His photographs have been on the covers of books by Michael Palmer, Thom Gunn, Keith Waldrop, August Kleinzahler, Norma Cole, W. S. Di Piero and others. He has also collaborated with many of the above on text/photo projects.